LOCAL FIRES

Stories

LOCAL FIRES

Stories

JOSHUA JONES

Borzello Trust Edition

(b) **theborzello**trust

PARTHIAN

Parthian, Cardigan SA43 1ED
www.parthianbooks.com
© Joshua Jones
Print ISBN: 978-1-913640-59-0
Ebook ISBN: 978-1-913640-60-6
Editor: Robert Harries
Cover Design: Syncopated Pandemonium
Typeset by Elaine Sharples
Printed by 4edge Ltd, Hockley
Excerpt from *Conundrum* by Jan Morris courtesy of Faber and Faber
Published with the financial support of the Books Council of Wales
British Library Cataloguing in Publication Data
A cataloguing record for this book is available from the British Library.
Printed on FSC accredited paper

Some stories first appeared in the following publications: 'Opportunity
Street' first appeared on the Common Breath blog (2021; RIP Brian
Hamill), 'Half Moon, New Year' was shortlisted for the 2021 Rhys Davies
Short Story Award and first appeared in *Take a Bite: The Rhys Davies Short
Story Award Anthology* (October 2021), 'Ten reasons why I didn't stop
Danny Jenkins from throwing your brother into a bin:' won third place in
Reflex Fiction's winter 2021 Flash Fiction Prize and first appeared in their
In Defence of Pseudoscience anthology (July 2022), and 'Who Are You
Calling Kim Woodburn?' first appeared in *Gutter No. 27* (February 2023)

Table of Contents

For Home

Brief Interview with Condemned Child #1

Why did you start the fire?

— You are talking as if you have already made up your mind. What evidence do you have that brought you to the assumption that it was us that started the fire?

You were seen running away from the church down Inkerman Street, shortly before smoke was seen trailing through the smashed windows, were you not?

— Were we? We were simply in the area. As I'm sure you know, I live nearby. So, you're saying someone saw smoke coming from the church, saw us chasing each other down the street, and put two and two together?

In my experience kids your age smash windows, litter, drink and smoke weed in the woods.

— In my experience, kids don't have anything else to do.

Except burn down a church?

— Except drink, take drugs, use up as much time as possible to pass through this nothingness so many of us feel. Why do you think so many of us are like this? Why do you think a boy in my year at school is currently in a juvie for dealing? Why is it that another boy from school, my age, was found dead in his bed after a night drinking?

Your guess is as good as mine.

— You don't need to guess. I'll tell you. It's because of this town.

Care to elaborate?

— This town breaks us. It is an oppressive state. A day here is a weighted blanket pressed down over your face, the suffocating darkness of it all. I realised this for the first time when six swans were found, on two separate occasions, with their heads decapitated and a stomach full of pellets from a BB gun. This senseless violence was very real for me. Very at home. Dad used to take me for walks through Sandy Water Park and point out the wildflowers, the seabirds. We haven't been since those swans were killed. A part of us died that day. Something broke.

Let's stay on topic.

— Have you read the *Mabinogion*? The woods next to the park are named after it, the sculptures hidden within inspired by its eleven stories. I remember when Dad took me there for the first time, and we hunted through the forest for the hidden sculptures. It was one of the best days of my life. Since then,

I've seen girls give head to boys they barely know in the clearing with the iron boar. I've seen people set fire to the boar, trying to melt it down. The sculpture of the owl, the stag also, both missing, the posts vandalised.

How is this relevant?

— There's no mystery anymore, Officer. And no reason.

The Fourth Wedding

I. Morning

In the room on the third floor, the pale, early-morning glow reaches across the walls, illuminating the interior, and warms the sock-clad feet of the figure lying spread-eagled on the bed against the one green-wallpapered wall.

She lies with her open mouth inches from a small pool of purple vomit, baring arse to the candelabra. Somewhere in the folds of the duvet a phone is ringing. Although muffled, its demands wake the figure. She stirs, her groans lost in the memory foam. She turns onto her side, cheek damp with dribble, wrinkling her nose in disgust. She smells the sick before she sees it and retreats across the bed. Pinching her nose, she searches with one hand through the duvet and finds her clutch bag by her knee. She fumbles with the lock and pulls out the phone from where it's nestled between loose change, receipts from the bar downstairs. She answers the call on the final ring.

— Alright Angie, love? Ow's the angover?

— Iya Jan. Am anging, fair play. You alright?

— Yes, yes, just downstairs with The Girls aving something to eat. Seen the time, love?

Angie squints through semi-closed eyelids, ignoring the dull ache in her left eye.

— Oh fuckin ell, it's half ten! Right, am getting up now.

— Don't worry, mun, we'll be up with some brekkie for you inna bit. What d'you want?

— Paracetamol and a Berocca if you got any.

— Yes, yes, no problem. Anything to eat though?

Angie unsteadily makes her way over to the desk above which a large rectangular mirror hangs on the wall. She curses under her breath as she almost trips over her boots and jeans strewn across the floor.

— No thanks, onestly. Angie pauses. Maybe some toast might elp though.

— Alright love no problem. I've got the keycard so you go sort yourself out and we'll be up inna bit.

She drops the phone onto the desk with a thud. Squints into the mirror, her nose almost touching that of her reflection's; her contact lens is stuck to the left of her pupil. The eye is bloodshot and sore. As soon as she starts poking at it, tears flood her waterline, threatening to cascade down her cheek, still damp with forgotten saliva. She extracts it successfully, flicking the discarded contact lens into the bin below the desk. She blinks away the tears, rubs at her cheeks with the back of her hand. She checks the other eye in the mirror and realises she must have taken the lens out after stumbling into the room late last night. You fucking idiot, she says to her reflection. Surely by the fourth wedding you know not to drink the night before?

The glass on the bedside cabinet is full of water. Someone must have left it there for her. How'd she get here? Maybe she wouldn't have thrown up if she had drunk the water. Or at least it may have washed out some of the purple colour. Angie picks the glass up and takes it to the en suite where she pours the lukewarm water down the drain. She fills the glass and drinks it in big quick gulps, soothing her scorched throat, and fills it again. She takes the glass back into the room and places it on the desk next to her phone.

Angie turns around to face the room and rests against the desk. She quietly observes the scene. Plans of how she's going to undertake the cleaning of the room are almost immediately discarded, long before they near fruition. The throbbing in her head is too violent for coherent thought. But, not wanting Aunt Jan and The Girls to see the state of the place, she kicks her discarded clothes under the desk. Angie drops the duvet and pillows onto the floor. Delicately, she picks at the corners of the bedsheets, brings them together and ties them with the vomit in the middle. Holding her breath, she walks quickly to the room door, almost tripping over the duvet and dumps the sheets in the hallway. That'll have to do.

The pressure of the shower drums against her scalp. It's hot and heavy, softens the dull ache in her temples. Standing in the bathtub, the curtain pulled tight across the flimsy rail separates this moment of solitude from a day giving vows of undying commitment. Weeks of practice. Flash photography, children dancing and crying, choking on a perfumed neck when greeting a friend or work colleague, relatives fighting over who has the biggest hat and who wears it better. Angie hadn't bothered with a photographer for the first two weddings. Well, the first one, they couldn't afford it anyway. But they hired one for the third; she thought it would be a wedding to remember. During the months of organising the fourth wedding, she had thought to herself: This, *this* is the one I won't want to forget. A voice through the front door, unmistakeably shrill, calls out from beyond the shower curtain:

— You in there, Ange? I got The Girls with me. Alright?

— Yeah, Jan, yeah. I'll be with you inna minute.

— No worries, love, take your time.

Angie washes her hair with the complementary shampoo, the air thick with the sweet smell of coconut. She runs conditioner through her hair with her fingers, pressing it into the tips. Some of the dye from her freshly blonde curls bleeds down her back and thighs; not enough to cause concern. She hums the tune of a pop song played on the speakers of the bar last night — what was its name? The lyrics of the chorus, a song her daughters knew and sang to each other, with their faces almost touching and giggling. The same ten, twenty songs played on loop all night. She had heard it three or four times throughout the evening, enough times to remember the melody, but didn't think to ask the barmaid who sings it.

Angie pulls the shower head from its clasp and washes out the conditioner from her hair. She watches the bubbles and creamy, coconut-scented foam swirl around the drain before descending. She briefly considers masturbating. Her water-wrinkled hand, still holding the shower head, skates past her considerable waist, past the caesarean scars and wide hips, towards her inner thighs. The water's hot, constant pressure is too attractive.

Rapturous giggling interrupts her moment. She opens her eyes and blinks quickly, the light fading through the shower curtain. She is suddenly aware of how long she's been in the shower and hastily places the head back in its clasp. Angie squirts shower gel into her hands and rubs it into her body. The artificial shea butter makes her almost retch. The faucet squeals when she twists it.

The persistent hum of the fan rushes to dominate the soundscape, without the whoosh of the shower to dampen it. White noise replaced by white noise. The curtain rattles along the rail as it's yanked back. She breathes in the humidity, imagines her lungs wetting, a relief from last night's chain-smoked cigarettes. She sighs, tugs a white towel from the radiator next to the shower. It's soothing against her forehead. She wearily rubs at her burning skin, rich red worn through the day-old spray tan. She douses herself with deodorant before covering herself with the white robe that is hanging on the back of the door. She takes another towel from the radiator and wraps it around her hair.

Standing in front of the mirror, Angie wipes a small circle of the glass clean with the side of her clenched fist. The fan has done very little to clear the steam from the mirror — it makes a lot of noise for something so useless. Which husband was that? Too many of them, really. She had a type. She prods the bags under her eyes. The skin around them feels puffy. She removes the engagement ring from her pruned fingers to rub cream on her face, quietly thankful for the neutral, watery smell of aloe vera and cucumber. Anything stronger would be opportunity for retching, in her current state of fragility. After tonight, with a new wedding ring on her finger, the engagement ring, with its rows of stones that smugly, expensively glint in the mirror-light, will be placed in a wooden box with red velvet lining, stored at the bottom shelf of her bedside cabinet, where the rings from previous engagements and marriages are kept. Before leaving, Angie scoops up the complementary toiletries and stuffs them into her makeup bag.

A heavy, perfumed fog envelops her as soon as Angie opens the door to the bedroom. Aunt Janet is sat in the chair by the desk, Angie's sister Susie and Charlie, Susie's daughter, both sit on the edge of the bed. Susie has a daughter and a son, both with the same father, from her first and only marriage. It still appears to be successful. Angie's own daughter Chloe, her youngest, stands in the back, between the bed and the window. The light from outside is still bright and fresh, not so pale as the morning. The aggressiveness of the ceiling light hurts Angie's eyes, still sore from sleeping with one contact lens pushed to the side like a nagging thought.

The Girls are loud, never listening, only waiting until it's their turn to drill into one another's ears with their incessant giggling. Their lips, ultra-pink, protrude from faces an unnatural orange that nears brown, startling against the whites of their teeth. Jan and Susie had taken Angie on a *girly date* to a teeth-whitening clinic in Swansea last week, before the hen party. It justifies the years of harm their mouths have taken, from drinking since their teenage years, and smoking longer still.

Chloe is different, despite Angie's attempts. The only thing Angie and her daughter share is their love for reality TV. Never interested in makeup, this morning Chloe allowed Charlie to put a small amount of mascara on her unusually long lashes. Her unremarkably brown hair is tied neatly in a bun on the crown of her head. She takes after her father; handsomely pale and tall. Husband Number Two. On this occasion, she had given in to Angie, allowing her to apply a very small amount of lightly coloured fake tan to her skin. She refuses to wear heels, says she doesn't need them — she's tall enough and holds herself in a way that is beyond her seventeen years. There she stands in the corner, quiet and graceful in a pair of sandals.

— Come sit by ere, love, Jan rises from where she sits and gestures towards the desk. Some Beroccas there for you an all.

Angie sits down and begins to pick at the toast. The butter is thickly coated, sludgy, the bread like stone. She drops a Berocca into the glass of water and takes a sip while it's still bubbling. The fizzling tickles her nose as she drinks.

— Chloe, have you seen your sister?

— She's just making sure the boys are okay, then she's bringing the dresses up, Chloe replies.

— Ohhh where the bloody ell have tho— found them! Jan passes the crinkling sheet of tablets over to Angie. Get two of those down you!

The pills feel like chalk in Angie's mouth and don't mix well with the fizzing water, the colour of a highlighter pen.

— How much do you remember from last night, Ange? Susie asks.

— How much do I want to remember? asks Angie, to laughter.

Charlie laughs too. She is still too young to drink, but Angie knows that doesn't stop people her age from trying to get into Met Bar with their sibling's IDs and their crop tops. She and Susie were those kids once, playing dress-up in each other's clothes and arguing over makeup. Most of their fights were over who borrowed whose shoes, or which boys were out of bounds.

Chloe sits on the bed opposite the open window, looking out with her back to the room. Outside the air is crisp. It has been a cold morning. A light breeze brushes through the neatly trimmed bushes and trees dotted around the courtyard. The car park a little further down the hill is mostly empty, except for a small number of vehicles belonging to staff. Mostly black, grey or white and all of them dirty, Aunt Janet's bright pink Fiat 500 sparkles in the morning dew. Square lumps of pink fluff in the shape of dice can be seen through the frosted glass, hanging from the rear-view mirror. It has been cleaned and waxed by Janet's new boyfriend the morning before. He always makes sure her car is the pride of the car park. On three occasions he has paid to have dents hammered out, the pink repainted, angry car owners appeased. Aunt Janet says she forgets she can't drive in heels.

The sky's usual grey is a pleasing blue, mottled with transparent clouds. The season could be mistaken for spring, if it were not for the wilting of browning leaves, like hands downstretched. Chloe watches the guests arrive, some of them parking cars, some of them walking up the bank, while her mother gets primed and ready to look like a star, as if she's about to climb the steps to the door of the Big Brother house. Though not before she's passed the wall of flagrant camera flashes by wordless paparazzi, invisible behind their cameras, the live audience bleating like goats. The gentlemen among the arriving guests hold doors open for their wives and the elderly. Children run ahead through the car park, their parents chasing after them, worried they'll dirty their hired suits and pretty dresses before the ceremony begins. Her mother's second husband didn't allow any children at their wedding. The entire day, she felt like something was missing. Since then, Angie's never had a childless wedding.

II. Night

Angie lies next to her new husband. The latest one in a series of men. Four of them made it to marital status; two of them became fathers. Of those married one became deceased, one divorced her, the other divorced by her, and the latest — yet to be determined. Downstairs, her son and first daughter, Bertie and Lottie, one birthed before the death of Husband Number One and one after, and Chloe, a blessing from Husband Number Two — or, as Angie sometimes refers to him, the sperm donor. They're still dancing, presumably. Jan and her new boyfriend hadn't been seen in a while. No one noticed them leave and even if they did, they wouldn't have cared. Bertie's waistcoat will be on the back of someone else's chair by now, its rust-coloured boutonnière missing. The cleaners will find it under a table in the morning, the dried aster flowers trampled and its orange petals missing.

Chloe had been too shy earlier in the afternoon to dance but, with Lottie's encouragement and the pushing of drinks across the white tablecloth by many an elder relative's tremoring hand, she found her courage. And then she kept going, stopping only to kick off her sandals or to pick up a runaway child and hold them in the crook of her arm while gently weaving her hips side to side. Strands of her hair fell onto her bare shoulders and one of the other girls would reach up and tuck it back into the bun on her head. Everybody adored her, all the young girls wanted to dance with her, and it made Angie's heart ripple with pride.

Peter rolls onto his back causing the bed to surge like a

wave, bringing Angie back to land. His belly protrudes from him like a barrel, his frame still wrapped in its wedding attire. Angie had given up the fruitless attempt of seducing him when he passed out, fully clothed, the lamps lit and swamping the hotel room in an aggressively warm glow. He was too drunk to fuck, although it was his idea to leave the party early. And not quietly either; not a quick dash to the exit and up the staircase. Angie would have taken off her shoes and held them by the strap as she let the carpet cushion her steps. No, not like that. Peter, being Peter, had bellowed over to Angie from where he stood at the bar, pint of Guinness in hand. Angie had been in the middle of teasing Bertie in front of his latest boyfriend with memories of him as a child, when Bertie was Bella. And how much Angie loved and supported him through it all, and how much she loved having a son. Bertie had his arm around his mother's shoulders, and the three of them were laughing, when Peter shouted *Right en, wife! Am finishing this pint, them am taking you upstairs forra shag!* Bertie scowled at him, and Angie rested a hand on his tense arm. *E's only havin a laugh*, she said.

Who's laughing now? Angie thinks, staring up at the ceiling. Peter had spanked her across the threshold of the room where she hoped they'd consummate their bond to each other. The room was dark when they entered, dimly light by the shaft of light from the hallway that threw Peter's wavering frame into shadow. Angie giggled, her buttock stinging from his mark, turned around to kiss him. He almost fell into her outstretched arms as he came towards her. She took him to the bed and laid him down on the covers, before dashing round the bed to light the two lamps either side of the headboard.

Satisfied with the *ambience*, Angie pulled herself on top of him. His stomach, like the hardened leather of a horse's saddle, had sweat through the Ralph Lauren shirt. She took to the task of unbuttoning him. The top two — no, three — had become unbuttoned throughout the evening, the more he drank. His chest lay bare under her thighs, displaying silvery curls of hair slick with sweat. His collar stank of spilled beer. She asked him to stay awake for her, just let her undress him, almost begging. He mumbled false hopes and empty promises. In the morning, he said drifting off; in the morning. He muttered something Angie had to lean in to hear, something about it being the best day, and tomorrow… tomorrow…

Wasn't this meant to be the best day of her life? What about the first three? Maybe she could have said that was true about the first wedding, to Husband Number One. It was unfair, his death. Unfair, she tells herself to this day, but she's forgiven him since. No, when Angie thinks about it, about the best day of her life, it has nothing to do with the weddings. She thinks of the day she took Chloe on a trip to London a couple of years ago, after Chloe had begged for weeks and weeks to visit the V&A Museum. She'd learned about Rodin's *The Age of Bronze* in school, looked at pictures of it on the internet, simply resolved she must see it with her own green eyes. And Angie said yeah, fuck it. She'd said yes for the shopping, and for that reason, they booked a private room in a hostel, so their newly bought treasures would be safe while they went out to a nice dinner. The next day was for walking around the museum, then a quick trip back to the hostel before the Megabus to Swansea, where Jan was to pick them up and take them home. They stashed rosé in the locker at the hostel, two bottles bought from the shop two doors down, before they headed to Oxford Street. Cheaper than drinking in London, Angie had said, ignoring the fact Chloe was too young to even set foot in pubs, except the ones in Llanelli, like Met Club and the Jailhouse, where any girl baring a bit of chest could get in without ID.

Shopping had been nice. They'd gone into all the expensive shops, the posh ones, looked at all the pretty things. They were excited for the Big Primark and what bargains they could score in TK Maxx. It had been a nice day. But that next morning, at the V&A, that was special. Not that Angie knew it would be at the time. She was there humouring Chloe. She'd loaded up on coffee first (and complained about the prices of sandwiches in Pret A Manger) and followed Chloe around the enormous rooms, feeling insignificant, listening to her daughter excitedly ramble on about Japanese textiles, landscape paintings by Amelia Long, who used to be a Lady of somewhere. Then into the sculpture room. The other stuff was alright, yeah, the art, but, Christ that sculpture. *The Age of Bronze*. How do you even describe something like that? It was beautiful. It emanated strength, and a fragility, that felt very manly. Or what masculinity should be — vulnerable. Its beauty was in its humanity. To be vulnerable is to be strong, or something. Angie felt very moved. She felt like she'd experienced something. She saw what Chloe saw.

Peter interrupts her thoughts with a fart. The smell follows moments after the sound, like thunder after lightning. It begins to rain outside. The patter of water droplets, apprehensive at first, taps against the windowpane, synchronises with the bass that continues to vibrate through the floors from the function room. Angie fills her lungs with air and lets out the deepest sigh she can muster until her lungs deflate. This is how I feel, like a deflated lung, she thinks. She gets up from the bed and takes a glass from the stand next to the TV. She carries it to the bathroom, holds a finger underneath the tap until the water, which rushes out so fast it feels like foam, is cold enough, and fills the glass.

On her return to the bedroom she places the glass gently on the coaster on Peter's side of the bed. She gently shakes him by the shoulders until he stirs, tells him to undress. She undoes the rest of the buttons of his shirt, and the ones on the sleeves, pulls it from his body as he lifts his head and shoulders off the pillow, his eyes closed, as if he's on autopilot. She unlaces the Hugo Boss Oxfords one after another, heaves them from his swollen feet — one, two, thr— She almost falls after the third tug. The shoe clatters to the ground to rest with the sole facing the wall. Angie unzips the fly of his trousers. As the buttons are undone his gut rises to fill the space. A rush of freedom. She slaps him on the stomach for him to pull his arse up from the mattress and she yanks them, followed by the Calvin Klein boxers, down past his thighs, knees, ankles and past the feet where the socks hang halfway, the body failing to fully reject them. Like a cheap piercing, or an ingrown toenail. His penis rests flaccidly on top of his testicles, comically pathetic under the looming, protruding belly, large enough to cast a shadow over the whole thing. Angie's hand rests on his shoulder for a moment. She reaches down, kisses him on the cheek. The rain is louder now, persistently hammering against the windowpane like little fists, drowning out the music from below. Too loud for quiet thoughts. Angie turns off the lights.

17

In the morning the sun shines sternly through the horizontal blinds. Angie turns her head towards the window with a groan, her eyes blurred and all objects undefined in her vision. She shields her eyes with her hand, the platinum band on the ring finger with its obscenely large diamond stones cutting off the blood flow. Underneath the patchy fake tan, the finger has turned a purplish grey, like a bowl of grapes left on the windowsill. I'm going to have to get it resized, she thinks. Angie squints at the window, at the figure standing there perfectly still, his penis resting between his thighs in the morning's cold embrace, his elbow against the windowpane. And his knee, his beautiful knee, crooked at just the right angle.

— Good morning, my love, he says. How's the hangover?

How Would Clive Owen Feel?

I've known for a long time, at the back of my mind, something is wrong with me.

I know it's wrong to say something is wrong with me. I've wanted to make this appointment for two years. It's taken me that long to build up my confidence, since I first started thinking about all this, since I knew I needed to speak to someone.

I never know how to talk about it, about feeling out of step with everything. So, I put this list together after speaking to Mam and Dad, and my friends. They've been begging me, all this time. A long time. And I've done my research too. I've been reading up about it, did some online tests and stuff. I know you shouldn't trust everything you read online. Anyway, I'll try to be quick.

I get hung up on the tiniest details when somebody's talking, especially in arguments. I guess I like to test people's boundaries. Sometimes I think I enjoy pissing people off. They say I'll go too far to prove I'm right — I've always... I just always need to know the facts, you know? And in an argument, I hang onto every word, like I want to catch them out. But I also avoid confrontation. I hate it. Oh, I take everything literally. This is something that really annoys people, especially my parents. They say the world isn't that black and white. And, it's like I can't understand body language, or sarcasm, or something. People say I'm difficult to read, like there's a disconnect between my facial expressions and body language, with how I actually feel. And it's so embarrassing when someone makes a joke and everyone laughs apart from me. I wonder what I've missed. Sometimes I need things explained to me. Sometimes I just laugh anyway. I don't get invited to many parties.

I struggle to make small talk or hold conversation. I hate it, unless I'm talking about me. I get accused of that all the time, just going on and on about me and what I like, and not listening when someone talks about themselves. I zone out a lot when people are talking. I can't help it. I worry I only care about me. And it's difficult to remain engaged with such a short attention span. I operate on something Mam and Dad call *William Time*. This is when a small task that takes two minutes to do will take two days or two weeks or two months. I'm not avoiding them — the tasks I mean — and I'm not lazy, even though everyone says I am. I just have a lot of thoughts that I can't keep up with. I started writing things down so that I'd remember to do them. Then I got obsessed with writing notes and sticking them to all the walls in the house, which drove Mam round the bend.

Oh, recently I've been getting really into reading Descartes' Dualism theories, because I like how they're based on mathematical logic and reason. It's like a factual way of thinking, which reflects the way I think. I got obsessed with the band Joan of Arc for a bit. Remember when I was really into rap-metal, Mam? A few years ago, I got obsessed with playing drums for about a month, Mam and Dad bought a drumkit and everything, then I moved on to the next thing. My current obsession is Clive Owen after watching *Children of Men* and now I have watched every Clive Owen film. I went to Coventry, where he's from — there was a Twitter account set up in 2015 dedicated to how much of a shithole Coventry is but it's only sent thirty-seven tweets, so I thought it can't be that bad? But the online comments aren't wrong, Coventry really is shit. And there are a lot of really bad Clive Owen films. Which has nothing to do with Coventry, but have you seen *Derailed*? It's so— yeah, sorry. You're right. I just mean that I get *obsessed* with things. Like, go down this really deep rabbit hole. I'll move on.

I can't even butter toast while talking, sometimes, or hold down a job. I struggle to multitask. There are times when I feel like I can't have genuine, long-lasting connections with people. I have lost so many friends. I panic on the phone — got better at that recently, actually. I just lost my job, they fired me after I had another breakdown. So, I've been applying for new jobs, been doing a lot of interviews over the phone. Just had to force myself to do it. I know I can't avoid talking on the phone, but I still try. It still makes me shake. Like I'm on an adrenaline rush, and the crash — it's a bad landing. Like, before a call I'll pace around the room, my palms damp and sticky. Then the call itself, I'll be totally fine, joking, small talk, asking questions. As soon as I get off the call, I just let out this big sigh of relief. This breath that I didn't realise I was holding. I don't know why I'm going into so much detail about this, sorry.

I often say things out of panic. I didn't mean them, I just didn't think. Maybe that's why people assume I'm being rude or mean all the time. Seeing people cry annoys me. Does that make me sound like a dick? Sorry, I keep swearing. It's the nerves. I try to hide my insensitivity — I just feel like I'm not empathetic, unless I'm extremely empathetic. I never cry. Seeing other people upset doesn't make me feel upset. But when I'm at the cinema, I can't keep the tears in. Maybe it's to do with being in a dark room?

You know, I feel like I want to throw up on the counter, just before I'm about to pay for something? I'll be waiting in line, thinking about how I'm going to word what I'll say, thinking about every sentence, working on the structure. I'll be waiting there, in the queue, planning small talk, with this feeling in my stomach, like I'm carsick. I think everyone does that — I don't think I'm a special case, not in the slightest. It's just, I feel like I need to say it. I've been wanting to make this appointment for two years and I felt — feel — like it's important to bring up my inability to put myself in other people's shoes. I want to be a writer, but how am I meant to be a writer when I can't understand how other people feel?

I'm almost done. I know this is taking a while. I want to talk about my senses, I have it written down. My clothes feel like they weigh a tonne. I usually avoid fabrics like silk and velvet — just touching them makes me feel sick. And I don't like being touched or hugged. I'm not being dramatic. It's a strong, physical reaction, I feel repulsed. My eyes burn when the light's too bright and my hearing... my hearing is crazy. Last time I went to the cinema I had to leave because I could hear feedback in the speakers and it stressed me out. My friend couldn't hear it. I can usually hear things that people can't or say they can't. It makes me feel paranoid at times.

I just want to look people in the eye without feeling awkward and to speak without stuttering or stumbling or forgetting what I'm going to say before I say it. I want to know what is going on. Throughout all my years of school I was *the weird kid*, I was *quirky*. It's embarrassing, it feels like having excuses made for you, like: he always looks that grumpy, that's just the way he is. Don't mind William, he's just like that.

So, what do you think? What's going on with me?

William looks up from the crumpled pages with his writing scrawled all over the front and back of them. He makes eye contact with his GP for the first time since sitting down in one of two plastic chairs lined against the wall. He folds the papers with shaking hands and puts them back in the breast pocket of his blazer, before wiping his damp palms on his trousers. One of his legs has been drumming a quiet beat against the laminate floor since he sat down. His mother sits in the chair next to him and has remained silent while William reads from his notes, encouraging him with silent nods and sad smiles. When he finished and looked up, she had taken off her glasses to dab at the corner of her eye with a tissue. She gently squeezes his shoulder with her other hand, ignoring his flinching.

The room is small and stuffy. The light hurts William's eyes. Its punishing glare fills the room, bouncing off the posters on the walls that warn the reader of the dangers of smoking, showing dirty, diseased lungs; of various cancers, of what to do when someone has a heart attack or stroke, the numbers for mental health helplines. Opposite where William and his mother sit is an examination bed in medical blue plastic and a curtain rail above their heads. The curtain itself is hideously beige, the colour of a bandage or plaster. Skin colour, people call it, like other skin colours don't exist. It's also factually inaccurate. Imagine people walking around with skin the colour and texture of a plaster. William can hear people walk past the examination room: the rolling creak of a pram's wheel, someone's jeans brushing as they walk. Muffled, disembodied voices fade down the hallway. On the wall to the right of William, between himself and Dr Kothari, is an anatomical diagram of a vulva, with little arrows leading to the names of all the different parts. William tries to keep his gaze firmly away from the poster.

— Thank you for coming, William, Dr Kothari says from behind his desk. He has a stern mouth but kind, reassuring eyes under his thinly rimmed glasses. William was relieved that Dr Kothari hadn't interrupted him while he had been reading from his notes, apart from to gently hurry him along. William had been researching body language, reading articles on his laptop into the early hours of the morning. He sees Dr Kothari's steepled hands are lowered in his lap, with one leg crossed over the other — this means he is listening.

— From what you have told me about what you are experiencing, I think you might be autistic.

William feels a strange tingling in his fingers, not quite numbness. He rubs his palms against his knees. Everyone had been right: there really was something wrong with him.

— I cannot diagnose you here and now. I will be referring you to a specialist who will be able to properly diagnose you. The waiting list is long, you may not be seen to for up to nine months, possibly a year. Possibly longer. I urge you to put it out of your mind until then if you can. It is nothing to worry about.

William's mother grips his elbow in support, and he doesn't flinch. He doesn't know what to say. He forces a weak smile and looks up at the diagram of the vulva, quickly looks down. He wipes his sweaty palms on his trousers again, his leg drumming furiously against the floor.

— I want you to know that this doesn't change anything. If you are diagnosed, which I am sure you will be, it does not change who you are. There is nothing wrong with you.

— Thank you, doctor. We needed to hear that, didn't we, Will? How do you feel?

His mother is looking at him through watery eyes. How does he feel? William isn't sure. Well, he feels a bit annoyed. Why is she crying? How would Clive Owen feel? His character in *Children of Men,* Theo, is stoic, strong. He doesn't show anyone when he cries, like when Julianne Moore's character, imaginatively named Julian, is shot dead. Julian is the ex-lover of Theo, and the mother of their dead son. After she is shot dead, he crouches behind a tree to smoke a cigarette, and breaks down in tears on the forest floor. William feels like crying. He wishes his mother and the doctor would stop staring at him as if through a microscope. He feels like a fresh wound, something grievous that Dr John W. Thackery, Clive Owen's character in *The Knick*, might operate on. Something foul and gaping under the harsh white light of a medical lamp.

Dr Kothari uncrosses his legs and begins typing at the computer. The clacking of the keyboard fills the silence between them and makes William fidget. His mother sniffles. Is she sad, or is she relieved? Dr Kothari pauses from typing and wordlessly hands her a box of tissues from his desk. She takes one with a quiet thank you and pats at the corners of her eyes, careful not to smudge her makeup, then blows her nose. The noise of it is intrusive. His mother blowing her nose, a sound so violent and yet so normal, feels alien in the sterile sanctity of the examination room. The same room in which any understanding William had of his own identity has changed with the same sudden force.

Opportunity Street

Jimmy Pugh marched down Opportunity Street with his fists clenched in the pockets of his leather jacket. He had been seething with rage, carrying it around with him like a padlock around his neck, since he read the news in the *Llanelli Star* a few weeks ago.

He strode past the Betfred gambling shop, lit up like an amusement arcade. Through the front door an old man could be seen with a folded newspaper, his hat pulled down over his eyes, circling bets on its pages with a red pen. And the Works, its yellow and blue storefront fighting for attention against the Barnardo's green. Jimmy knew the guy behind the counter at Barnardo's; he had one arm and a short temper.

He passed the hairdressers with its pretentious window tint, the shadows on the other side of the glass with their heads in basins. Shadows that stared at their own reflections in the mirrors, their bodiless heads balancing on satin gowns. There were empty units on both sides of the street; big, white cubes, house lights beaming, waiting for purpose. Jimmy rolled his shoulders to ease the tension simmering under the skin, the tendons stiff and rubbery, and stared at the brand-new sign above the door of his destination, with an intensity that could burn a hole through the PVC: GARY'S FIREWORKS.

How fucking dare he! A vein throbbed at Jimmy's temples. It was thick and it writhed, pulsed like a worm. He could hardly think straight. The worm nibbled at his thoughts, leaving only the angry and violent ones. The fun ones. His clenched fists were beginning to sweat in the leather. A bloody good sign, that. Bold. In your face. Dominant colours. Who the fuck does Gary think he is?

The shop was nestled between an antiques dealer on one side and a YMCA shop on the other. There were house plants, violently lush, in the windows of the flats above. Mannequins wearing military jackets and Brodie helmets stood next to dark wood dressers adorned with binoculars, compasses and old, yellow newspapers in the windows of the antique shop. One of the mannequins held a rifle in its hand. Probably a replica, but just as likely not to be. A man lounged outside on a green velvet desk chair, his feet resting on a box filled with old film cameras and lenses. He was smoking a cigarette, reading an instruction manual on how to fly a Spitfire. The man seemed to not notice Jimmy, or the sign next to the door to the fireworks shop that read GRAND OPENING TODAY! in gold paint. The 'O' in OPENING was stylised to look like a Catherine wheel. Tacky. Such a good sign outside as well. There were banners and balloons strapped across the door and tacked onto the walls and windows. People walked down the street with their Bags for Life and their eyes fixed on their feet. Jimmy watched the man as he flicked the ash from his cigarette. Why's he reading a book on how to fly a plane? Maybe he was hiding something.

Despite the unusual warmth of the October air, Jimmy's leather jacket, bought on holiday in Kuşadası — real leather, as real as the mannequins' rifles — was zipped to the chin. Through the window of the fireworks shop were people, customers, drinking from flutes and browsing the displays. He scanned their faces, looking to see if anyone was trouble. Nothing out of the ordinary.

A teenage boy in a smart shirt, with a fringe and acne scars, stood behind a table at the front door. He asked Jimmy if he would like an orange juice or apple, or lemonade. Jimmy seized two flutes, one of apple juice and one of lemonade, to simulate cider, a trick he'd picked up from others attempting sobriety. He downed them both, one after another. He looked over his shoulder at a woman, standing in the doorway with a young girl, presumably her daughter, waiting for him to move further into the shop. She seemed to be looking at him with something akin to repulsion. Or maybe she was attracted to him. He winked at her just in case.

Jimmy barged his way into an aisle behind an elderly couple who were moving slowly, dithering over various brands of sparklers. He sucked air through his pursed lips, held himself at his full height, over the crooked backs of the two. Their wrinkled hands clasped each other's, their heads jutting out from their bodies, like frail little birds.

— Do you think these ones are safe for children?

— Ohhh yes, love. I'm sure they are. What about these ones? Perfect for her bat mitzvah.

— Hmmm, I'm not sure. What about these—

— I wouldn't get those ones for a bat mitzvah if I were you, sorry to butt in.

The corner of Jimmy's lip lifted slightly as the elderly couple jumped and turned around to see who was assaulting them from above.

— Yeah, those aren't great for children at all, really. Don't

want em to burn their little hands, do you? Tell you what —
he grappled with his jacket's breast pocket, the pocket too
small for his shovel-like hand — come down to my shop and
I'll sort you right out.

He thrust a crumpled business card into the elderly man's
free hand and pointed to the address in blue Comic Sans font
under the badly photoshopped image of a fireworks display.

— That's the shop there, Station Road Fireworks. Come
down to see me and I'll sort you out with a bunch of sparklers
the kids'll love. He leaned in, as if to share a secret: they'll be
cheaper than in here, too.

They thanked him and bowed their birdlike heads. Heads
that could be crushed in Jimmy's hands. He watched them
amble their way to the door.

— Hey Jimmy, Jimmy!

Jimmy turned around to see Jon from the other side of the
shop, so impossibly thin he glided through the gaps between
groups of people like a wraith. They stood there, idling,
discussing their plans for World Teacher's Day and
Halloween, speaking like they were reading from a script
about their summer holidays, and how great it was to get away,
even just for a weekend/a week/fuck, two weeks — someone
went on a cruise, a fucking cruise, for months, MONTHS! —
and how the women in Shagaluf are really something, and the
men with children laughed, their wives at their elbow, and
drank their room temperature orange juice while wondering
how different their lives would be if they didn't have children,
who they surely love very dearly, that were conceived on the
back seat of their first car, a Ford Fiesta, or something equally
as shit — maybe they would have known for themselves how

fit the women are in Magaluf. And they could afford to go on cruises, and someone pulled them out from their thoughts when they asked them what fireworks they were thinking of buying and they replied with oh, I'm not sure, really, not sure what I can afford, with it being Tom's birthday next week, and the conversation moved on, to health insurance and how the indoor market is dying and — who smells like sausage rolls? — and—

— Jimmy! Hey, Jimmy!

Jon was now in front of him, holding out a glass of orange juice. He had a sausage roll wrapped in a Greggs paper bag jutting out of his pocket. The space between their bodies, Jimmy's stocky ex-bouncer-type build and Jon's stringy limbs, the ones that children yelled oi! Slenderman! at him for in the street, smelled of hot, sticky sausage meat. The hand holding out the orange juice was shaking. Jimmy knew the shaking.

— Alright, Jon. Sorry, I was in my own world there. Alright?

He declined the drink.

— Yeah, am good, Jim, am good. Not drinking anymore, haven't had a drink in a while. That's good, innit? The AA helps. Gary comes too. I think he gets a lot out of it. It helps, yeah. I had a slip-up though, mind, yeah—

— Ah, sorry, Jon. Sorry about that.

— Yeah, you know, was my birthday last month. Was on the non-alcoholics, you know, but fuck, couldn't help myself. Fucking weird though, since trying to quit I've had a proper craving for salt!

He pulled the paper bag out of his pocket; the pungent sausage scent wafted into Jimmy's face. Jimmy could taste apple juice and pork-flavoured air on his tongue. Jon took a bite and, between chews, he said:

— I wanted to ask, I hope you don't mind Jim — are you still selling spice?

Jimmy lunged in, on his tiptoes, right up to Jon's ear, the lobe dangling above his mouth like bait in water, waiting for a fish to catch itself. The smell was repulsive. Fucking repulsive.

— Shut the fuck up, mun!

— I was only—

— I don't sell that shit anymore. I can't afford to get caught. It's illegal now, you know that, don't you?

Jimmy sunk down onto his heels, away from Jon's dangling earlobe, and looked around the room. No one seemed to have noticed the interaction. Someone beat the air with a fireworks price list. Wait, is that her? No, can't be. He waved the sticky air away from his face. The sausage roll scent was making his eyes water. He blinked, wiped his eyes with the back of his hand. Jon was looking at him over the rim of the paper bag. The woman he'd winked at and her child were looking at him. Were they looking at him? The worm in his head was quivering. A couple near them were whispering, Jimmy saw their lips saying:

— It can't be wise, can it, opening a firework shop just three weeks after that bloody fire?

— Aye, I know, I know. Bloody daft.

Are they looking? They're looking. His fists in his leather jacket were clenched, sweaty. The smell of sausage meat felt like it was clinging to his skin. He turned back to Jon.

— But you know where to find me if you want any weed.

— Yeah, thanks, Jim, sorry for asking. See you later, yeah? Gary's bout to do a speech now, I think.

Jon slinked away through the gaps of people in their threes and twos, as Jimmy turned away to the displays of fireworks along the wall in their glass cabinets. There were Solar Storms, Pink Dawns, Blue Skies and Frontline Fires, Red Tigers, Purple Tigers, Thunderbolts, Avalanche Thunders, Ghost Riders and Spitting Cobras, mines and streaks and rockets, Angel Dust, Acid Rain, Sky Dragons, Phantoms, Whistling Waves, and Skybreakers, Hell Raisers, Phoenixes and Griffins, Supernovas, War Hawks, Hell, Eden, Zeus, Moon Lights, Angels and fountains, ammo packs, fucking Catherine wheels, Black Cats, Stealth Boys, Jibber Jabbers and — fuck, are those Beasts? And Demolishers? FUCKING RETRIBUTION?! His thoughts thrashed in his temple, each one burning like a coin left in the sun. How could Gary afford this shit? Who's his supplier? How fucking dare—

A cheer rose up around the room as Gary made his way to the front of the shop, shaking hands and smiling as people patted him on the back. He stood there, smiling, the smug prick, between the cashier's desk and the crowd. A small mountain of a man, waving his hand above his head self-consciously as the crowd continued to clap, smiling at — why the fuck is the *Llanelli Star* here? They weren't there when he opened his shop! — smiling at Mr Owen's camera, blinking fast in the aftermath of the flash. Mr Owen let the camera rest against his ribs on its strap and poised ready with his notepad and pen to catch every word.

— Alright, alright, thank you, thank you! The crowd ceased their clapping. Thank you for coming and supporting this new venture. Bit different to plumbing, innit? He grinned. Twat. Now, I'm sorry to get deep here, but I just wanted to say, and I'm being honest here now, I wouldn't be here without my boy — come here, Iolo! The fringed little shit with the acne appeared at Gary's side, with his mother and his God-awful posture teenagers have these days— and my lovely wife. Without them, I wouldn't have gotten sober. He's fucking loving this, isn't he?

— Without them, I wouldn't have gotten sober and I wouldn't be in a position to open this shop. And yeah, it's a struggle, and it's hard when you see your friends dying from their addictions, and your family suffering with your own. It's fucking hard. Did he rehearse this? But I'm here, I'm healthy, and I'm sticking to sobriety. The crowd cheered and clapped. Jimmy clapped too. He didn't want to look like a dick.

Jimmy lingered near the wall, fingering a box of Retribution. Jon was over by the door, licking crumbs from his fingers. People helped themselves to more juice, resumed their conversations about... oh, who cares—

— Din't think you'd make it out, Jim.

— Ah, well. Here I am, aren't I?

— Been drinking?

— You know I've been trying. You know, getting it together. Yeah.

— You look like you should be drinking. You look like shit when you're drinking, somehow you look worse when you're not. What's all that about, Jim?

The worm was burrowing in his brain. He felt motion sick. How a fish probably feels when they fall headfirst down a waterfall. Do they know they're about to cascade off the side?

— This shop is the shit, the real deal.

— I know, Kim. Look, I'm worried. I'm not doing very—

— No one gives a shit about our end of town, Jimmy. Take it from me. I had dreams of setting fire to the café every night. Now, I'm free. You could be free too. You could actually clean yourself up if you let go. Anyway, I'll see you. I'd say it's been nice, but.

He watched his wife's back as she spoke a goodbye in Gary's ear, then left the shop. She had squeezed the prick's arm before she left, that was definitely a squeeze. Are they fucking? How's he going to sell his fireworks when he's got this much competition — competition from a legitimate business at that — and on Opportunity Street! Christ, Nando's is just a stone's throw away. And the Odeon and the Hungry Horse. Jimmy's going to get all sorts of foot traffic. Who even goes to Station Road anymore? It's fucking dead, nothing but spiceheads and takeaways, it's—

— Jimmy! So glad you could come. You got my invite, then?

A hand pressed into Jimmy's and squeezed it. The hand, attached to a wrist and an arm covered in hair so blonde they appeared hairless, and as white as a threadworm, belonged to Gary. The stubble on his head was indistinguishable from that on his cheeks, chins, neck. The hand was dry, the skin firm and thick. His fingers bore the feeling of hands so callused from years on a trade that they never fade away, becoming as much a part of the hand as fingernails, or knuckle tattoos.

— Jimmy? You there?

— Gaz! Yes, sorry. Not sure what happened there. Were you saying something?

It was too hot. Why was it so hot? Too many bodies. Too many worm sacks.

— Yeah, yeah, I was just saying it's good to see you, Jim. Been a while, am glad you could come. How's the shop?

Jimmy pulled him over to the opposite wall where there were fewer people, fewer bodies. He fully unzipped the leather jacket.

— Can barely hear myself think! Quieter over here. Good turn out here, aye? Fair play to you.

— Yeah, innit! Could say it's gone off with a blast, eh? Wink. Gary nudged with an elbow.

Fucking knob, with his tiny eyelashes. Why's he winking. Walked right into that one. Urgh. How quickly could he kill Gary before someone pulled them apart? He saw a film the other night where the main guy killed someone with a pencil. I could do that, Jimmy had thought. He could smash Gary's head into one of the glass display cabinets, force a rocket down his throat and light it. He'd pick up that brat and spin him round by his fringe and use his body as a weapon. He'd find a pencil, he'd—

— Ha, yeah, good one, Gaz. Smile. He coughed up some phlegm to try and wet his tongue. His teeth were sticking to his lips. So, Gaz. Cough. What licence have you got on this place?

— Oh, you know, thought I'd go for a long-term licence. See how that goes, first. See if we have the trade for it. It means we can do birthdays, weddings, gender reveals all year round!

— What the hell is a gender reveal?

— Yeah, you know. Blue fireworks for boys, pink if it's a girl. Got blue or pink sparklers and confetti rockets too.

— What the fuck is the point of that?

— Yeah, I don't know. Business though, innit?

Fuck. He's right. Jimmy's head felt like all the juice had been sucked out and squeezed to get all the dregs. He was sweating, cooking in his jacket, but the zip was undone, and the black Fred Perry knock-off polo unbuttoned. He licked the sweat off his upper lip. It tasted of apple juice and gunpowder.

— Oh, Gaz, I wanted to say, those are some nice knuckle tatts. When d'you get those done?

— Aye, pretty cool, eh?

He lifted his fingers for Jimmy to see and wiggled them in his face. Jimmy resisted the urge to bite them off, one by one. The black ink on the skin glinted in the ambient LED lighting. Stubble dotted the Olde English font that spelled out LIVE LIFE across the eight digits, the 'f' partially disguised by the simple wedding band.

— Got these done a few weeks ago. Just thought it made sense you know? I've stopped drinking, and opened this shop, and I got thinking. I realised that when you're on the bottle, you're not really living, are you? And that's what I want to do: live life. He looked over at Jon, leaning against the shop window. Maybe we can do something about him too, eh? Are you alright, Jim?

The worm throbbed at his temple, boring in under the skull. It had sucked his blood dry and left behind a thirst. He was a fish who'd caught the hook, and was now gulping in the air above the water.

— Gaz, am gonna have to go. Got some stuff to do. Good luck, yeah?

Jimmy staggered in the direction of the door, leaving Gary

surrounded by boxes of colourful packaging advertising explosives for family-friendly entertainment and discounted offers on seasonal holidays, and people who had run out of juice and now were quietly raising questions — out of earshot of Gary — of pints.

The air outside the shop was cooler now, the sun crestfallen behind a pocket of clouds, the streetlamps not yet punching in for the night shift. The worm howled from under his skull, there was no moon. His vision was blurred at the edges. The house plants in the windows of the flats above were black, their razored palms cutting a threatening figure from their nooks. The man outside had disappeared and so had the furniture. The antique shop was empty, bar two mannequins in the window, naked and missing limbs. Their blank faces watched Jimmy stumble out onto the street. He looked back at them, and the fireworks shop, and its door was closed. The lights off, window papered with tattered advertisements for a circus, a local talent show at the theatre. His ex-wife's face bleached and peeling. The PVC sign above the door of the shop that once boldly spelled GARY'S FIREWORKS in gold paint was faded, most of its letters missing. A pastiche of mail lay under the letter box. There were no people, no celebrations. Nothing to celebrate. The windows of the hairdressers were black, reflectionless. Through the windowpane of Betfred's door Jimmy could see the old man from earlier, sat in the dark and slowly circling bets in the paper. The strip of starless sky visible between the parallel rows of shops converged on Jimmy, their smashed-glass cobweb formations looming large. All the units were empty. House lights hanging from a wire, the drywall ceiling panels black with mould and crumbling.

The Episode Where Homer and Marge Sleep with Danger

I hoped we'd get a chance to talk. It's so good to see you again! How long has it been? Too long, I don't know. You've got kids now?

Old Flame:

That's amazing, I could never.

OF:

No, honestly. I know people say that all the time, but I really mean it. Feels a bit weird to bring a child into a world where there's so much shit, you know? Mass unemployment, no one can afford to rent. Forget ever buying a home. I don't know, there's plenty of kids needing to be adopted, so maybe one day.

OF:

It's so good to see you again! So long since I last saw you, and I can't even remember the last time I saw Amy. I wish we hung out more, before we all drifted apart. We're here now, aren't we? Did you invite her to your wedding?

OF:

Why not?

OF:

[...]

Doesn't matter now, anyway. When I found out she died, I just started thinking about all these memories from school, like the night of your fifteenth birthday. Do you remember? You had a party at your house. Both your older sisters had moved out by then. You never mentioned it, but I got the impression they didn't speak to your parents. Are they still not speaking?

OF:

Still don't? Fuck. That's a long time.

OF:

Chelsea was there, at the party. She wouldn't shut up about all the blowjobs she's given. She was always banging on about that sort of thing. Amy and William were there too. I remember Chelsea brought vodka and no mixer. That always did your head in. *How we going to drink that with no mixer?* you'd say. Amy brought a pack of alcopops with her, the cheap ones. The green one always reminded me of the bar of radiation Homer drops in the *Simpsons* intro. I never drank them, because I thought they'd make my piss the same colour. Amy didn't talk much all night, she never did. She sat there in your bedroom against the wall, sipping her pops, looking up at Chelsea as she banged on and on about boys. William didn't bring his own drinks, as standard, but Amy didn't mind sharing hers with him. She was always so kind, wasn't she?

OF:

Your mother was fucking terrifying. I'm sorry, I won't lie to you. I never was a liar.

OF:

Does she still call herself a Wicca? A Witch of the Light, or whatever. Such bollocks. Is she here?

OF:

Oh, God, I'm sorry. I honestly didn't know. I would have been there if I knew. But you know what I mean — she made voodoo dolls! It's weird, I've been thinking about that shed she kept next to your stables, and that plastic greenhouse. She grew stuff to make creams and ointments, didn't she? *We haven't been to the hospital in years!* she would say. Whenever I complained about an ache or pain from playing rugby, she'd give me a little pot of cream to take home with me. And it actually helped! Sometimes she'd ask if there were any dead friends or relatives I'd like to contact. I'd always decline. Even after my grandad Tommy died.

OF:

Your dad was always sound. Still is in fact. I had a nice chat with him earlier. It's good to see him again. I should buy him a drink. How's he been without your mam?

OF:

Yeah, I bet. He still walks like he's just got off the saddle. Bloody hell, those tattoos on his arms are blotches of ink now. I can just make out the dragon below his elbow, look, and the Celtic cross. He told me once, you know, he used to have tattoos across his knuckles, before he got them removed. I asked him about them once, when I helped him muck out the horses. He told me had the birth dates of your sisters laser-removed, did he ever tell you that? I wonder what hurt more. [...]

He whipped up a cracking buffet for your birthday party. I still remember it now — that's how good it was. Not that my parents didn't feed me or anything, but do you remember how much of a bad cook my mam is?

OF:

At your birthday party there was a really decent homemade pizza with loads of cheese, and one without cheese for Amy.

Cheese gave her the spews, I remember that.

OF:

There were mini sausage rolls and a fuck-off bowl of chips as a centrepiece. Every party there would always be a massive bowl of chips for everyone to help themselves to. Have you been to the buffet table yet, by the way?

OF:

Seen the size of the bowl of chips?

OF:

Yeah, you're right, maybe it is a bit weird to be thinking about food after a funeral. Amy would have loved all this though. It's just nice to see everyone coming together like this, you know? At your birthday party there was salad with lettuce, sweetcorn and carrots, all from the garden — your mother piled it on her plate with her hands — and homemade coleslaw. And a tonne of sandwiches, all cut into perfect triangles. It's one of the things I miss most about living in Llanelli and being young. I seem to remember a lot of birthday spreads.

OF:

These days it's mostly wedding dinners and funeral buffets.

OF:

[...]

Chelsea ate like one of your dad's horses. I can't get the image out of my head. I was a skinny kid then. Do you remember how skinny I was?

OF:

Yeah, proper scrawny. It's been a while since I didn't have to think about what I'm eating! I'd put it away and never gain any weight. You used to say you wished you were like that.

OF:

Amy didn't eat much that night, which was weird, and she didn't touch a slice of the cake. But he wrapped up a few slices in a napkin for her to take home. He always looked after her, your dad did. Your mother doted over William, offering him this and that, making sure he had ice cream with his cake, asked him if he was okay for a drink. I was never asked — she never really liked me, did she. No, honestly. I know she didn't. We played Drunk Jenga that night, no one knew any card games. Chelsea wanted to play Spin the Bottle. *Who's going to kiss you, Chels?* you asked. *You can't kiss him* — me — *because he's with me, and you can't kiss Amy* — *unless you want to, Ams?* Haha.

OF:

She just shook her head and laughed. Do you remember the rules of Drunk Jenga? I haven't played it since Freshers'. Feels like ages ago, now. I remember you had to have a drink in one hand at all times. Down your drink if you drop the tower, that sort of thing. And there were rules written on the bricks, like *Make another player choose Truth or Dare, pick someone to down their drink.* You pulled out a brick that read *Kiss the player to your left.* You made a big joke of asking me if it was okay. It lasted just a few seconds, Amy put a hand to your face, and I always thought the way you placed her hand back on the carpet was so gentle.

OF:

Do you think it meant more to her than we thought?

OF:

It's possible. I mean, we always knew that she was into girls, even if we never said.

OF:

She must have thought we'd stop being her friend or something. I wish we'd told her that we were there for her. Even Chelsea, even William were there for her.

OF:

Although, William just looked moody when you and Amy kissed. When did he ever not look fucking moody? I think he fancied her, you know. Or maybe he fancied you?

OF:

I can't believe he's not here today. He should have been here.

OF:

[...]

OF:

I remember, later on, when the game started to become boring, Chelsea got one of those Truth or Dare bricks. You said *Dare*, when it was put towards you. *Go and have sex with Gav!* she said. Christ, I swear she almost pissed herself with excitement.

OF:

I can picture your face now, a shade of red that had nothing to do with how much you'd had to drink. William seemed to be grinding his teeth. Chelsea poured us vodka shots, for luck or something. We never spoke about it, after it happened, did we?

OF:

The last thing I remember before shutting your bedroom door is a bag of overflowing beer bottles and empty cans, and how grey Amy looked. Imagine how much your mam would have kicked off if she heard us creeping into the spare room!

OF:

I remember first thinking this room was a guestroom, with its white, neutral walls and sheets and net curtains. Then I realised it had probably belonged to one of your sisters. Still, I led you to the bed and kissed you, but I don't know, it felt different.

OF:

Did it feel different to you?

OF:

You had braces then and they kept banging into my teeth. I didn't mind. When I went to take off your T-shirt, you stopped me. Remember? Do you? You asked if we could just sit there and talk.

OF:

We were shivering. I hadn't noticed how cold it was in that room until we were sat on the edge of the bed, feeling a bit awkward. Looking back, I should have said something more concrete. Or anything at all.

OF:

I should have said something like, that's absolutely fine. Or, we don't need to do anything you don't want to. I must have been pretty useless.

OF:

Because you asked if I didn't mind. You kept apologising. But honestly? I was relieved. Neither of us was ready. I should have said so.

OF:

I'm so sorry.

OF:

I went to draw the curtains, but you said no, keep them open. *I want to be able to see you,* you said. You went to lay on the bed, and I followed — I don't know if you remember this, but I almost headbutted you when I tripped over the rug! Such a mood killer.

OF:

So embarrassing! We laughed it off. I can remember it all so clearly. You don't mind us talking about this do you?

OF:

It's not weird? You sure?

OF:

I know it's a bit weird to talk about at a wake, but I don't know. I'm feeling sentimental. Do you want a drink? I'll get you another drink.

[…]

[…]

OF:

They didn't have Coke so had to go with Pepsi. That's a double too, by the way. Where was I?

OF:

Ah, yeah. I remember we talked for ages, like we are now. You said that, earlier in the day, Jupiter could be perfectly seen in the sky. You explained to me what meridian meant. What was it? Hang on, it'll come to me.

OF:

[…]

Fuck, I've forgotten. It doesn't matter. You were obsessed with astronomy, anyway.

OF:

You still are? That's great! I'm glad. Some things don't have to change.

OF:

When we re-entered the room, Chelsea and William were there with the TV on, an old episode of *The Simpsons* playing on Sky. Homer and Marge were hiding from a storm in a barn and were now having sex in a hay loft. Isn't it weird I can still remember that? Chelsea said Amy was chucking up in the bathroom. Massive shame — Amy loved *The Simpsons*. Chelsea asked us what happened, and you said that we did have sex.

OF:

I'm glad you lied. I've always kept it to myself.

OF:

William's face, he couldn't clench his jaw any tighter!

OF:

He didn't speak to me for the rest of the night. You could see why people thought William was an arse, but you said he's alright once you get to know him. I knew you took pity on him. Everyone made fun of him. You were like that, just nice to everyone.

OF:

To be honest, I never liked him much.

OF:

Oh, come off it! You knew I didn't.

OF:

The week after the party, I asked the boys in school if what people said about Chelsea was true.

OF:

They said she'd sucked off at least half the rugby team.

OF:

Even Danny Jenkins, they said.

OF:

I heard Chelsea is a caseworker now. Isn't she working with kids with mental health problems or something?

OF:

I'm really happy for her. I'm glad she managed to sort it out. It's a shame she couldn't be here.

OF:

Amy would have wanted her here. Fair play to Chelsea's mam for coming. And it was so nice of your dad to help out with the food — what a lovely spread it is!

OF:

I was nervous about coming home, about seeing you and some of the old gang. I'm glad we could talk. Danny Jenkins is still a prick though, isn't he? I bumped into him in the pub the other night, off his face he was.

OF:

Do you know why William isn't here?

OF:

[…]

It's good to catch up, and to talk about old times. We were so young, then. So stupid. I've been thinking a lot about that birthday party, when you and Amy kissed. I think it meant more to her than we realised. We shouldn't have brushed it off — I don't know, I feel stupid, but… Maybe she'd still be here. We should have said something, said it was okay, you know? I hope she can be herself now, wherever she is.

[…]

OF:

Yeah, it's been nice to see you too! I should probably mingle, catch up with people. Stay well. Look after yourself! And… yeah.

Half Moon, New Year

— Get off me! Get the fuck off me!

He lies in a crumpled mess amongst shards of smashed glass and cigarette butts. Spilled booze drenches his skinny blue jeans. Makes it look like he's pissed himself. Maybe he has. The pocket of his white shirt is ripped and hanging by a thread. He's holding his hands up in front of his badly beaten face, the hands scuffed, palms embedded with grit. His brow is bust open and the cheekbone a swelling plum. There's blood rushing the gap between nose and upper lip. The bottom lip is torn up bad too. His head is turned away towards the floor. He spits out a bubble of snot and blood, a subtractive mix of yellowish green and bloodstone red. The bubble bursts before it hits the ground. Danny Jenkins is pulled away from the boy on the floor by a mass of hands and screams. Disembodied voices howling, What the fuck! Get off him! They sound far away, obscure. He stops trying to kick the boy and tries to find his feet on the alcohol-slicked floor.

It was raining and had been all night, chattering on the roof over the beer garden. Weather doesn't stop the drinking. The girls, in their skirts and makeup, flirt with the boys, squeeze up to them for warmth and a packet of crisps. The boys in return don't mind. They roll cigarettes for the girls — who don't want to smoke, not really, but maybe it'll warm them from the inside — asking them how the hell can they roll with those massive fake nails? The boys whose parents can afford to buy them expensive winter coats wrap them around the shoulders of the girls. These coats are SuperDry and The North Face, the shirts Ralph Lauren or Levi, or else they wear River Island T-shirts a size or two too small to show off the muscles they're trying to develop. These muscles are filled with water and protein shake, but the girls say, Yeah, they're massive. Look at you. You look huge. And so, so strong.

No one wants to admit they're cold. They all start the night hugging their knees or with their arms crossed in front of their chests, huddled as close as they can to the dented patio heaters without making their discomfort apparent. They drink their pints quickly, so their teeth won't chatter. Many of the girls can keep up with the boys, and the boys know it, but not all of them like beer or cider. Some of them want cocktails, with real fruity flavours unlike the artificial blackcurrant in their Strongbow Dark Fruit. But they can't afford them, especially now with Christmas just gone. When the boys offer them a drink, they choose what they want — what they actually want — and savour it. Boys make fun of boys for drinking cocktails, or any drink that isn't piss-coloured. Call them ponces. No one cares, though, not really. It's all jest and festive spirit. It's *banter*. And as the night goes on, the girls inch away from the patio heaters, their cheeks tipsy-flushed under their blush. It's New Year's, and it beats being at home.

It has been a pretty good night. The corrugated plastic roof, in all its bird shit and glory, keeps them dry. Plus, the sound of the rain helps to construct an atmosphere where people feel cosy. While the boys just sort of stand around, talking about the Scarlets vs Ospreys game and whatever else boys talk about, the girls open up. Talk about Christmas dinner and Boxing Day leftovers, happy younger siblings and Pandora rings transition to — as the girls lean against each other on the wooden benches — conversations of family arguments and tensions at home. One girl complains about her bratty younger sister who threw a tantrum because she didn't get a Crosley record player. And another girl's dad is, like, a total dick when he drinks whiskey, and he'd started drinking really early, before lunchtime, so by the time dinner was ready he had a look on his face, you know? And the gravy wasn't right, and the roasties weren't crisp enough, and Mum was in tears. And that night he sat at the table, alone, drinking, while everyone else's families sat around the TV or playing games. Here, the girl chokes back a sob, and the other girls cluster around her, dabbing gently at her tears so she doesn't streak her mascara, and she tells them that on Boxing Day morning she woke up to find her brand-new house plant, a Christmas gift, with its stems snapped in half.

This is the scene inside the Half Moon pub: older men and women sit around rickety tables with sticky tops, perch on stools around the bar, couples around the pool table, their children at home, not mentioned. The TV is on, next to the darts board, the BBC presenter standing in front of crowds, the London Eye behind her, describing the atmosphere as electric, and lively. When a man goes outside for a smoke he nods at the young people, says something like:

    — Bloody cold, innit? You having a good night?

    — Yeah, good thanks, yeah. Yours?

— Sound, mate, yeah. Sound.

And he stands in the doorway, listening to the jabber, puts out his cigarette and goes back in without saying a word. Or if it's an older lady she chats to the girls, says how beautiful they look, just bloody lush they all are, and the girls invite her to sit with them and she says, Don't mind me, love, don't mind me, and clip-clops back into the warmth. When the countdown begins the young people rush in and they all stand there, everyone intermingled and chuffed, arms around shoulders. They cheer and clap as the fireworks go off over the Thames in HD and the music plays. Everyone downs their drink and sings Auld Lang Syne out of tune, and no one knows the words, but it doesn't matter. A few tear up then and laugh it off, say they get emotional when they drink, but really, they are glad to have made it another year. And the new one will be a good one. They know it. They'll wish it into existence.

This is where Danny comes in through the heavy front door, another boy holding him up, both sodden and dripping and freezing cold. The other boy looking vaguely pissed off, the sort of look that says he's not having the best night but is trying to salvage it. And Danny, Danny is fucked. His eyes hard and unfocused, his jaw clenched, unclenched, clenched. Everyone turns to look at them as they come through the door, the way people do when anyone enters a room. Danny tries to square up to them, unable to focus on anyone. His friend smiles, embarrassed. Their trainers squelch as the floor sticks to them and they cross the bar. The friend orders two Cokes and the barman asks, Is Pepsi okay, yeah? And the friend says, Yeah that's fine, whatever yeah.

By now the room has regained its composure. The music

flows and so do the drinks. The atmosphere is merry and celebratory despite the two boys bursting in. There are toasts of *Iechyd Da!* to health, to family, to the new year. Someone challenges another to a game of pool as they rummage through their pockets for a 50p coin for the table. Danny slumps over the bar and his friend pulls him up by the shoulder. Makes him sip the Pepsi, apologises to the bar staff when he slaps the glass down hard and sticky, cold Pepsi swamps the gnarled wooden top. No one says anything. They don't want to upset the mood.

The young ones trickle out into the smoking area and the cold, resume their positions around the patio heaters. Arms and legs folded, toes curled in their boots and heels and trainers. Cigarettes are slowly rolled by hands red-raw, the paper licked by tongues sneaked past chattering teeth. Everyone's sufficiently drunk enough now to freely complain about the cold, all bravado melted away. Danny and his friend had followed them out to the smoking area. The friend thinks the fresh air might clear Danny's head.

— Alright? Mind if we join you? the friend asks, sheepishly.

They say of course, join them! They all converge closer together on the already coveted bench space. And the boys ask him if he saw the Boxing Day rugby match. Danny glares into the middle distance as if to pick a fight with thin air, aggressively silent and saying nothing as the friend discusses the tries and penalties and performances of individual players.

— Hey Dan, what do you reckon of Samson Lee's game? the boys ask, trying to get him involved.

His jaw clenches, unclenches, clenches. He says nothing, staring at something no one else can see.

— Not very talkative tonight, is he? one of the boys says in a taunting tone.

The friend quickly picks up the conversation to fill the awkward space. He sits as near to the heater as he can, his knees touching the metal base. His shirt is damp and he shivers, chains cigarettes for warmth. When the conversation lulls, one of the girls asks the friend where's he been that night.

— We went to Spoons first to meet up with our mates, but it went pretty dry pretty quickly. It's cheap yeah, but who wants to drink in a pub where there's no music? The others nod in agreement, take drags and sip their drinks. Someone goes to the bar, someone else offers to go with them. Two of the boys are having a heated discussion about this year's John Lewis Christmas advert. Danny sips his drink, the glass loose in his hand.

— So then we all went to Met Bar and that was alright.

— Must have been packed, was it?

— Proper packed, yeah, stood out in the rain for ages waiting to get in. But yeah, it was good. Decent atmosphere and all that. But then we had to leave cause we got chucked out, thanks to this one here. He jabs a thumb at Danny, who is now glaring at the friend.

— Why? What'd he do?

— Knob as usual, had to start a fight, didn't he? Had to leave then, thrown out by the bouncers.

— Fuck off now, isi? Danny says to the friend.

The friend shrugs, downs the dregs of his drink and gets up to go to the bar without asking Danny if he wants a refill. The girls turn around and begin talking between each other, feeling uncomfortable in Danny's presence. He slouches with his back against the brick wall, making no effort to ease the tension in his muscles.

Two boys and the friend return from the bar, their hands like claws around the glasses clutched to their chests, spilling foam and laughing. People come and go to the toilet for a piss or to do a bump. There's a smash followed by a euphoric wave of *Waheey!* from inside the pub. One girl says she has to go, her mum's waiting up for her, and all the other girls get up to kiss her on the cheek, say they'll do something soon, before she goes back to university for the next semester. There are hugs and lots of *Happy New Year's, babes*. Someone, a boy, offers to walk her home, but she says she only lives a street away. And then she leaves through the smoking area, into the car park and down the road. Danny's friend sits down with a pint and silently hands one to Danny, holding it in the air while he finds his unsteady grip. They sit in silence, not facing each other. A girl gets off her phone with a *Fuck sake!* and jams it into her clutch bag. One of the girls closest to her asks:

— What's wrong, babes?

— Can't get hold of Big Dave again, mun. I know it's New Year's and he's busy, but he said he'd be here an hour ago.

— Ah, fuck, that's annoying. I'm running out too.

Danny's friend overhears the conversation and pauses mid-roll, a cigarette filter in his mouth.

— You talking bout Big Dave? I've got some here if you want?

The two girls come over to where Danny and the friend are sitting. The boys watch them, annoyed that the girls would rather give them attention. One of the older men, stood in the corner with a smoke, turns his head but doesn't say anything.

— Shhhh! A little quieter, yeah?

— Right, yeah, sorry. Do you want some then?

— Aye, go on, ta. Car park?

— Let's go for it. You coming, Danny? The friend asks.

Danny shakes his head, his face like uncut stone. He watches the friend and the two girls make their way through to the car park, stepping over feet and handbags, saying they'll be back now in a minute when someone asks them where they're going. Someone asks Danny if he's alright and he nods once, takes a big gulp of lager. The friend and the two girls crouch behind a car. Danny can't see them except their heads, but he knows the friend will pour a sliver of coke from the baggie onto his knuckle, then he'll offer to do the same for the girls, as if to be a gentleman, but the girls will take the bag from his outstretched hand and pour their own quantity. It will be a small amount too, as to not take the piss, but maybe a little more than the friend's portion, to help see them through the night. They lift the knuckle to their nose and close one nostril with their finger, and all at once they inhale, in comradery.

When they return, they're rubbing their noses with the back of their hand, stretching the skin around the bridge with their fingers to ease the sinuses. The friend plonks down on the seat next to Danny, grinning widely. There's a new intensity in his eyes, the muscles around them hard. The friend pulls a packet of gum from his pocket and slips a piece in his mouth. He makes sure the translucent bag of white powder is firmly sealed. Danny silently, slowly, lifts a finger in the air. The friend looks at him. Danny says nothing, looks him in the eyes. The friend is chewing the gum in a frenzy. He pulls the bag back out of his pocket and unseals it, holds it out to Danny, who dabs a finger in the powder, then lifts it to his mouth and rubs it into his gums.

Conversation resumes, and Danny eases up, joins in. When someone says they watched the *Home Alone* films for the first time over Christmas he says, What the fuck? You've never seen *Home Alone* before?! And when the girls talk about New Year resolutions, about wanting to start back at the gym and try a new fad diet, try to shift some of the Christmas weight, he says, Nah, no need. You're fit as it is. They say thanks, laugh dryly, shift uncomfortably in their seat. Danny shrugs it off. He offers to buy the friend a drink, the first time since they arrived at the Half Moon. And Danny goes off without offering to buy anyone else a drink. The friend sits back in his seat, relaxed but intense, eyes darting back and forth from face to face and ears tuning in and out of the conversations around him. His stomach is churning but not in an entirely bad way — yet, this next drink will have to be the last.

Danny reappears in the doorway with two full glasses in his hands, walks across the decking and next thing the friend knows, Danny is on the ground. The glasses smash on impact and the sweet smell of cider fills the air as the golden liquid and foam flow into the gaps between the planks of wood. There's a cheer of *Waheey!* from inside the pub. The girls scream and everyone in the smoking area jumps at the sound of glass smashing, and the mass of flesh and fabric slamming the ground. They lift their feet and bags off the floor onto the bench, so as not to be soaked in the spilled drink. The boys laugh in unison, a chorus of cruelty.

The friend and one of the girls rush to help Danny to his feet but he's up before they can get to him, his cheeks flushed, lips pulled back over his teeth. And before anyone can stop him he pulls his fist back and socks the boy closest to him on the jaw. Danny grabs at the boy's shoulder and punches him in the stomach, once, twice, three times, four. Danny wrestles the other boys off him with a strength that has built through the night from the drinking and the drugs. There are screams and shouts to get off him. There's a sound of ripping cloth. The boy is shouting. Get off me, get off me! He tries to push Danny back so he can get a punch in but can't, Danny hitting too fast and too strong. The boy curls up on himself, his hands in front of his face. Danny pushes the boy's hands away, the bundles of arms and hands unable to keep him from the boy. There's the sound of knuckles hitting soft skin and muscle. The boy's cries of pain and shouts for Danny to stop. Two girls are sobbing. One of them starts beating on Danny's arm and pushing him but he doesn't notice. Danny's face is frozen in a snarl, his eyes stony. One of the boys pulls the girl away, tells her to not get involved. Danny starts to tire, and the boys manage to pull him back, but not before he knees the boy in the stomach and drops him to the ground.

— Get off me! Get the fuck off me!

The boy lies in a crumpled mess amongst shards of glass and cigarette butts. Spilled booze drenches his chinos. He's holding his hands up to his nose, eyes scrunched up in pain. His brow is bust open and the cheekbone already beginning to swell. There's blood rushing the gap between nose and upper lip, soaking into the collar of the boy's shirt. The bottom lip is torn up bad too. He turns his head towards the floor. The blood pools among the grain of the wooden decking. Danny is pulled away from the boy on the floor by hands and screams.

Disembodied voices howling what the fuck! Get off him! They sound far away, obscure.

— The fuck, Danny? What the hell you doing?

— The cunt fucking dropped me! I know he did! He stands there, his chest rising and falling, drenched in sweat despite the cold.

— No one dropped you, you fucking idiot. You tripped and fell!

— Nah, fuck off. He did. I saw him put his foot out.

— Danny, no one tripped you up, you freak! one of the girls shouts at him.

He turns to face her, his hands still tightly balled into fists.

— I'm so sorry, everyone. I'm really sorry. He's been like this all night, I'm fucking taking him home, I'm sorry.

The friend grabs Danny by the shoulders and pushes him to the door, apologising the whole way. Danny doesn't put up any resistance, shocked faces following them. There's a boy with a dustpan and brush and a puzzled look on his face, who squeezes up against the wall to let Danny and the friend push past. The friend pushes him through the pub so quickly no one has a chance to get a proper look and wonder what the bloody hell is going on.

The air in the smoking area had been thick with cigarette smoke, the inside of the pub stuffy with bodies emanating heat, packed from wall to wall, the radiators on full blast. Out here on the street, the air is so cold it burns Danny's split knuckles. It begins to rain again, with him and the friend on the doorstep of the Half Moon. The rain drips through a hole in Danny's jeans. Must have happened when he fell. His palms are grazed and sting in the cold. The friend won't look at him. His head is pounding.

— You're a prick, you know that, don't you?

The friend is breathing heavily, on the verge of shouting. Danny doesn't answer, bends down to inspect the badly bleeding knee through the hole in his jeans.

— That's it then? Just not gunna answer me?

Danny sighs, his brain beating a drum against his skull. He looks across the roundabout outside the pub, at Capel Als church that looms over the road, separated by a cast-iron fence that may have once been painted gold but has now faded to a sort of beige. He remembers trooping down the hill as a child in primary school under the guidance of their teachers, uniformed under their little coats, to sing Christmas carols at the chapel. Danny and his friend would sit in the balcony, singing the carols and hymns in silly voices, like Darth Vader or Batman, under their breaths.

— Do you remember when we were kids?

— The fuck you on about now, Danny?

— Do you remember when we were kids, and always had to sing there, every Christmas? Danny points at the chapel. Those were the best days of my life. Simpler then, innit?

He lets his hand drop to his side. Laughter and music come faintly from inside the pub, a car beeps its horn in the distance. The rain, falling heavier now. He looks up and blinks away the rain.

— Shame there's no stars out tonight.

— I can't be fucked with this, Danny. I'm done. Go home, will you?

Danny watches as the friend disappears down a turning. He

begins to walk up the hill in the opposite direction, past Capel Als, the warm glow from the Half Moon's windows fading with every step. He wonders if the friend meant what he said. For the first time that night he notices his shirt is soaked through, with rain mostly, sweat and alcohol too. There's blood on the collar and the cuffs. He shivers, hopes his Mam had remembered to turn the heating on, even for an hour.

Tommy

I grew up inna two-up two-down in Speke. When I was four years old, maybe five, we moved to the estate from Anfield. I remember me Da wasn't made up. A bunch of em lost their jobs down the docks. Aye, 1959 it was. In the two years before we moved to Speke, Da an his pals gambled on whatever they could. The footie, horses, dogs. It got heavy. Christ, it's all coming back to me. My memories are hazy when I drink, like breath on a window. There are things I don't want to remember, but I need to do this.

There are these pictures that tick away behind my eyes; a projector on the fritz; Mam slapping at me Da with a tea towel, him rummaging through the drawers for stuff to pawn; Da coming back from the job centre, breathless and parched. I can hear Mam's aggressive silence. Her cousin said he could land Da work at the airport. She was up the duff with Vicky at the time, she was at her wit's ends, you know? The airport was still being built so it meant he'd keep a job for a bit, keep him out of trouble too maybe. So, he got a job there, an you should've seen him the day we left for Speke. He made his way through a fresh packet of cigarettes in the taxi. He had a funny way of smoking. He'd suck the smoke through the gap in his front teeth and blow it back out through his nose. This is one of my strongest memories of the time, this. It's like a reel of Super 8 on a loop. He was in a strop the whole ride, because she'd confiscated the bottle of rum he'd hid between the door of the car and his seat. Mam was too good to him then, before she got ill. They were setting up betting shops everywhere back then, right next to the pubs. She saw it all.

Da left the gambling in Anfield but he took the drink with him, wherever he went. And, you know, I guess it became apparent that I inherited Da's thirst, and me Mam's depression. When Mam got ill, he lost himself a bit. He had booze knocking about everywhere. He didn't realise when some of it went missing. Every morning I made us sandwiches and walked Vicky to school, already a bit sloshed. When Mam was well she was proper. She made our lunches and Vicky was always clean and her hair brushed. The more ill Mam got the more dishevelled Vicky became. I skipped out on footie after school to wash clothes and brush Vicky's hair. The boys thought that I was helping Da around the house. I was so embarrassed.

At sixteen I left school to work at British Leyland until it closed a year later. Then I went to work at Ford, because my manager from the old job liked me and saw how good I was at fixing up cars. Before he reached me when doing his rounds I'd cob into a rag, make the exterior sparkle. I was into the Beatles at the time, and drinking. Aged eighteen I'd stay out late, smoking in bars, listening to rock an roll, getting into fights with dock boys. It was normal, no one realised there were problems, you know? Everyone had problems.

Our uncle Mikey lived across our house on the estate. He had followed us from Anfield. He took me on as an apprentice carpenter after I lost my job at Ford for drinking on the job. Everyone drank on the job, I was just the one to get caught, sod's law. I was slower than the other boys in school but good with my hands, Uncle Mikey saw that. We was off, working outside on warm days, us and the radio. It was Tears for Fears, Gary Numan and New Order then. Skaghead music, Da called it. Didn't care, nah, made me love it more.

It wasn't until the early eighties that I began to think about leaving Liverpool. After a few years learning the trade from my uncle, I was off. Twenty years of handling baggage had eaten away at me Da's soul. I'd had enough. Dad drank until he was out of this world. He raged in short bursts, just to retreat back into himself just as quickly. It was too much to bear for Ma. So I packed my bags and that was that. Vicky was old enough to look after herself and I sent her money when I could. It was Sheffield at first, then Leicester, Nottingham, Norwich, Southampton. All over the bloody place. I had a cassette player and a bag of tapes and that was it. I was drinking the whole time, of course.

Every new town meant new bars and new drinking buddies. Getting hammered with a bunch of strangers, promising you'll do it all again tomorrow, and then you never see them again. That was my religion for ten years. By the time I got here I had worked in Cardiff and Swansea. I loved Wales and decided it was time to put my feet up. I was getting old and struggling to keep up with the younger lads. The people were friendly and the drink was cheap! Llanelli was alive then, do you remember? It was better then. That was when I met my Cath. I was mad about her. She could put the drinks back, matching me pint for pint in those days. But she knew when to stop. After a year of dating and drinking we was married and we have been since. Our kids, Junior and Liz, they've had their kids now. I love em all, you know? It's mental being a granddad. I love kids, but I can't be around em, stinking of booze all the time. Hiding booze in me sock drawer, under the sofa. It got really bad when Cath found vodka in the toilet cistern. I was hopeless.

I lost my job about three years into the marriage. I was always drunk, but never sloppy with my work. And I was proud of my work. But I started drinking heavier and heavier, falling asleep on the job, making mistakes, until one mistake became a disaster. And then they found I was taking drink with me in my lunchbox. But did that stop me? Nah, course not. I got fired and then stopped looking for work so I'd have more time to drink. Then Da died, and it was just me and Vicky, who barely talks to me anyway, not since I left her. It was all a bit much for me.

I guess I'm here because I want to learn how to say sorry and mean it. I'm sorry to Vicky for abandoning her. I'm sorry to Cath for the stress. I want to be a part of my grandkids' lives. I don't want to fuck up again, you know? I want to take the kids for fish and chips, or treat Cath to a nice dinner, and not fuck it up.

Tommy rubs at his eyes. As he unloaded he felt like he had become heavier, like his clothes have soaked up all the rain in a downpour. The garden of memory is the front lawn of an abandoned house, detritus snatched in ropes of thorns and weeds. Not a walk in the park, all this. He yawns so widely his jaw trembles, his back arches with the weight of a deep breath. He pushes down on both knees to get up from his chair with a small groan and pushes his knuckles into the small of his back.

Tommy hears a quiet crack through his fingers and feels a little lighter.

David unclips the wad of papers on his clipboard and slips the page of Tommy's notes at the back. He snaps the papers back. A fresh page, a fresh story.

— Thank you for sharing that with us, Tom. It's not easy being so open and sharing something like that in a group.

— Ah, it's nothing, Dave. Thanks for listening, everyone.

— Who wants to go next, then? Maggie?

— Do you mind if I step out for a quick ciggie? Could fancy some fresh air.

Tommy walks over to the coffee table while pulling out a pouch of tobacco from his jeans' back pocket. Only crumbs scattered across the bare wooden surface are evidence of there ever being any biscuits before Gary polished them off. Broken, interlaced coffee rings on the table reflect in the light, slowly drying, like an uncertain Olympic logo. Tommy rolls himself a cigarette, dropping small flecks of tobacco onto the table among the soiled polystyrene cups and unused napkins. He jams the filter end between his dry lips and pours water into a cup from a jug.

The wind has picked up since just a couple of hours ago. Tommy struggles to push open the fire door against the gust of air that whips through the widening gap between it and the frame. He steps through the door and closes it behind him. The plain wooden cross bolted to its front looks down on him piously as he tries to light his cigarette. The front gates of the job centre opposite are padlocked shut. The street is empty of people. One For Sale sign after the next. The bins to one side of the stone garden overflow. Pigeons pick at grey slivers of chips until a couple of seagulls drop down and bully them to leave.

Tommy's hands are clammy on the flint of his lighter. He wipes them on his jeans. He looks at the gulls fighting, the stone garden. He can't remember the proper name of it, if it ever had one. Not an actual garden, just a large circle leading from the pavement to the park, with benches made up of large slabs of stone around the circumference. There are cemeteries more pleasing to the eye, but looking at and thinking about the stone garden is distracting him from the York Palace, just a few doors down. He sees one of his drinking partners standing outside, his creaking leather jacket, as always, zipped over the barrel of his gut. Tommy must have known his name once. The man raises his pint glass to him across the way in friendly greeting. The golden liquid sings to Tommy, more beautiful than any birdsong.

The wind picks up, seems to be blowing in the direction of the pub. The clouds threaten rain, like the weather wants him holed up in a warm, dry corner with a drink. Cupping his hands to shield the lighter's flame from the wind, Tommy thinks about what he could cook for Cathy tonight. Something hearty, slow-cooked, something that says *we'll be okay, I'm sorry, I love you*. The sparks flicker in the wind but don't catch light. He gives up trying to light the cigarette. He leans into the wind, and begins to walk home.

Under the Belt, Above the Bed

— I'm between bodies at the moment. You know what I mean? Yes, you know what I mean — stop fidgeting — I look down the landscape of a body I don't recognise, this breastless torso. A snail trail leading down to a penis I feel entirely apathetic towards. Hairy feet — like that bear, sat by the bar, I bet he has hairy feet. But other times I put on a little makeup, see my ass in the mirror, I think I'm worthy of desire. I'm serious! Inside of this man's skin is a goddess with curls of ginger hair, tight thighs, hips that know the rhythm to every Beyoncé track. To be, or to become, a woman is the ultimate goal worthy of my entire dedication, don't you think? I cannot be a ghost inside myself forever now, can I.

Bertie taps the base of his fork against the side of the table as Sonny talks. This is the second time he has met Sonny outside of their drag persona. They're both two drinks in, enough to make Bertie feel slightly turned on when Sonny fingers the silver chain, the slight red indention mark on their soft throat. Sonny is wearing black trousers, their amber T-shirt tight on their chest, suggesting a slim, worked frame — hard collarbones like golden sand dunes at a holiday resort. From the kitchen, the sound of smashing plates.

— Yes, I know what you mean. I'm currently between homes. I'm moving to Bristol; all my stuff is in boxes. My tenancy finished last week and my new one in the city doesn't start for another two. It's a peculiar feeling, this transitory space between two definite points. I'm not homeless, but I'm not on solid ground either. I'm not secure.

Bertie stops to chew on the paper straw in his glass, his spit turning it to pulp in his mouth.

— I trusted my transition because, although I was floating in the grey matter between the societal definitives of gender, I felt like I was moving towards a point. Ah, and here's our food! I'm starving.

— Sorry about the wait! Had a bit of a disaster in the kitchen.

The waiter, purple mountains instead of eyes, speaks through an excellent customer service smile, his tail wagging. He gently sets the plates down on the table and trots off, tea towel sticking out of his trouser pocket.

— Handsome, isn't he? Sonny says, looking intently at their plate. He reminds me of the cockapoo we had when I was a baby. Well, I was too young to remember, obviously. But I've seen photos.

— He looked very tired.

— Why the city?

— Pilgrimage is a queer tradition. Would you like any vinegar?

— What does that mean?

— It means, how can I be trans and queer in a place like this? There's nowhere to dance.

— Is that true? Hmm, don't answer that.

— There's no joy to be found in this town.

— I think you're probably right. Wow, these are really good chips. Crunchy.

— A lot of queer people, they grow up in villages or towns like ours and don't even know any other gay or transgender kids. They think they're alone, until they go to the city, and there's entire clubs, streets where there's people like them. They can dance, get fucked, fall in love. Be shown there's a way of living past shame and beatings.

— Did you get beat? Sonny asks, through a mouthful of onion ring.

— Not really. Bertie sighs, wiping his damp palms on his trousers. Some of the other boys would hit me with a belt in the changing rooms, but only because I never reacted. I never cried out or made a face, so they did it more. I think, if I told them it hurt, they would have stopped. For some reason it felt important to make it seem like it never hurt. Ah, childhood! Memories as seen through a gauze curtain. How's the steak?

— A bit tough. I'm still not over the fact you took me to a pub called The Hungry Horse for a date. Not a single horse in sight. Lots of dogs though. We may as well have gone to Spoons. God, look at that family of ferrets over there.

— What would you have preferred? I had vouchers, anyway.

— You charmer! Somewhere nice. The Thomas Arms, perhaps.

— Full of rugby dads and estate agents? Pigs? No thanks.

— I suppose you're right. You're lucky I'm not classy.

— How's your meal? Can I get you anything? The waiter appears behind Sonny's shoulder. His tightly curled hair flops over his ears.

— How about another wine? Sonny asks, looking at Bertie.

— Sure, a rosé. I'd like something sweet.

— I see what you mean about the cockapoo thing, Bertie says, when the waiter leaves to fetch their drinks. When did you think you might not be the gender you were born with?

— Ah, yes. A good question.

— For me, it was when I stayed at an older man's home in London, Bertie says, watching Sonny fiddle with the ring on their middle finger. He was a friend, we had met at parties. He would drive us to the beach sometimes, to sip tea from a flask and watch the swimmers. He had a house in London he had bought when he used to be a TV celebrity. I just noticed how tidy your cuticles are. Very neat.

— What was the house like? I bet it was gorgeous.

— It was a beautiful house, fucking massive, these really tall ceilings and bare wood floors. The living room was painted entirely dark green, even the radiators. The hallway was like the inside of a cherry. God, look at that woman's dress! Someone's getting laid tonight.

— Oh my God, yes. That colour!

— We had fun, at first. I listened to his stories about sharing cigarettes with John Cooper Clarke back in the day, coffee with Ken Russell. Every story involved a namedrop. Half of them I didn't know at the time, I was too young. He didn't mind. I think he wanted me to be impressed by him.

— Ew, pretentious! Hmm, not sure how I feel about this wine. Not very sweet.

— He smoked a lot of weed, I tried to keep up. I started feeling dizzy, heavy-headed, you know how it goes.

— Oh, it's the worst, Sonny says, crunching an ice cube between their teeth.

— I don't smoke weed, I get anxious. I began to feel very

anxious. I was sweating. He asked me to stay in his bed that night. I panicked, staggered up to the room I was staying in and barricaded the door with a chair — bit of an overreaction, but I thought I was about to get butt-fucked by a seventy-year-old has-been. The chair had sat in front of a closet, keeping its door closed. I moved the chair and the closet swung open, and underneath these long, fur coats were women's boots in a pile, and sharp heels. I played dress up, and as I flounced and pulled poses in front of the mirror, I swear I felt my anxiety leave my body. For a moment, I was a woman. I fell asleep that night, I swear I was floating above the bed. In the morning I thought nothing of it, decided not to. But on the train home, and for weeks after, I realised what I wanted to be. Would you like my lemon?

— Oh, no. I don't do bitter, babe.

— So, what about you?

Funnily enough, it was under a belt. Have you ever read any Jan Morris? Hang on, I'm just going to get a napkin.

Sonny, a giraffe in heels and skinny legs, moves to stand above the rest of the animals at the bar. A cow with a not-there stare and a leather jacket sucks peanut mulch from behind a tooth filling. Sonny is used to being gawped at. Their chin never tilts down, unless addressing someone shorter than them, such as the bartender, an otter with whiskers and a straight mouth. They return to the table, carefully dabbing the corners of their mouth with the napkin.

— She was a transgender travel writer from Wales. She started her transition in the sixties, then underwent gender reassignment surgery in 1972. She's lived as a woman for decades. She was a member of the first British expedition to climb Mount Everest, and travelled to every country you can think of.

— You have such lovely ears.

— What?

— Oh, nothing. Just absorbing.

Sonny rummages in their coat pocket for their lip gloss.

— She wrote, in her book *Conundrum*, that she recognised her 'incessant wandering as an outer expression of her inner journey'. What are you trying to express by moving to Bristol?

— This again? Can't we just enjoy our night?

— Who says we're not enjoying our night?

— Ah, well—

— I want to know what you're running from.

They use their phone's front camera as a mirror, begin applying the lip gloss.

— I'm not running from anything, like I said. I'm running towards something.

— Yes. You think there is freedom of gender at the end of the rainbow.

Sonny smacks their lips together.

— And the end of the rainbow is always in some city. Every city looks the same to me. Page 20 of *Conundrum*: 'gender is not physical at all, but is altogether insubstantial. It is soul, perhaps, it is talent, it is taste, it is environment, it is how one feels, it is light and shade, it is inner music, it is a spring in one's step or an exchange of glances, it is more truly life than any combination of genitals, ovaries and hormones. It is the essentialness of oneself, the psyche, the fragmentation of unity.' God, I wish those ferrets would stop looking at us.

— Do you always quote entire paragraphs from books on a date, or.

— Only when I'm on a date with someone cute. Oh, stop blushing. Look at them look at us! You carry gender, and ultimately your own freedom, with you. You can have it right here.

— Yeah, I suppose, I—

— Do we not have that, right here at this table?

— Why have you not fully transitioned?

— Define 'fully'.

— Ah, I'm not sure I can.

— Does transitioning have to be binary? If male and female are two distant train stations, then I am on the train in between, on some never-ending journey, enjoying the scenery. I'm comfortable with my fluidity. It's not that I don't know who I am, it's that I am in constant exploration of myself. It's like a relationship where you're learning something new about your partner, all the time, and you feel yourself growing with them.

— I'm sorry, I've upset you, haven't I.

Sonny holds Bertie's chin, presses a manicured thumb softly to his mouth.

— Oh, hunny. You couldn't upset me if you tried. I'm happy in my inbetweenness, and getting to be Stacey Sinnamon when I want to. I was thinking of creating a drag king persona too, A Sonny Afternoon. What do you think?

— It's a good name. It's a little cute, for a king. There's a lot of power in a name. I felt that power, when I got my new passport, with my new name. Funny how it took legal recognition for me to finally feel like I could exist the way I want to. I had my family's acceptance, the support of friends as I began my transition. I read about attacks on trans people on my Twitter feed, institutional hostility. And yet, I didn't feel secure in my transness until those same institutions recognised my existence as a trans man.

— I don't want you to go to Bristol, Sonny murmurs into their wine glass.

— You can be honest with me. You'll miss me. Do you want anything from the dessert menu?

— I like having you around, yes. And no, we don't have enough time. Oh God, look. Another smashed glass. That's the third one tonight.

— I wish I felt at home in Llanelli. In Wales, even. The truth is, I've always desired leaving. Sometimes I feel like I desire leaving more than I desire the place I'm going to.

— Jan Morris moved back to Wales when she began her transition. She felt like it was appropriate, to be at one with her spirit, solitude away from Oxford, London, the rest of the world, and to 'say goodbye' to her maleness. She belonged here, she found the people kind and accepting of her. Why can't you?

— Because the Welsh are the ones who have called me names, beat me with belts, who said I couldn't possibly be a man, who forced me to hide who I am.

— That's not a Welsh thing, it's a people thing. You'll find hate in Bristol too; people are fucking animals. More of it, probably — bigger population, more risk, even if there are also more spaces and more of an understanding. Oh, shit. My tag is beeping.

— Do you need to head home soon?

— Yes, curfew. Well, I have had a lovely evening.

Sonny reaches round the back of their chair and begins to pull on their wool coat. They motion for the bill.

— Shall we split the bill? You never told me why you're on a tag.

— Ah, yes. Well, I battered a policeman. The night of the talent show, actually. Went out afterwards, and as I was walking home from a bar, I got jumped by a couple of fucking blobfish in tracksuits. I tried to defend myself. A police car happened to be driving past the street, the rat bastards got out and pulled the boys off me, but tried getting me into the back of the car. They said I must have asked for it somehow, so I bolted him in the face. Couldn't run in heels though, so here I am, on tag. I shouldn't have drunk so much wine tonight, I feel a bit drunk!

— Do you have community service tomorrow? Ah, the bill, thank you Cockapoo Waiter. Actually. Don't worry about splitting. I got this.

— I'll get it next time. And yes, I'm at Oxfam tomorrow. It's fine, I can pinch things for my costumes.

Bertie lightly kisses Sonny's knuckles.

— I feel bad for talking about how good it felt to be recognised by the government, when you're here, getting into fights with the police.

— My love, from where I'm sitting, we're both very beautiful right now. Oh God, this thing is really beginning to beep now.

— This place is a fucking zoo. Let's not notice them, as they watch us leave. C'mon, let's get you home.

Brief Interview with Condemned Child #2

Why did you start the fire?

— For fuck sake, I didn't! We didn't! How many more times do I have to tell you?

Swearing at a policeman can get you in a lot of trouble. Well let's face it, you're already in a lot of trouble.

— For something I supposedly did. Yeah, great. Don't you have anything better to do than harassing kids, or is that part of the job description? There are county lines, gangs from Newport, from as far as fucking Birmingham, London and Liverpool and turning this town into the wrong kind of market town. There are teenage boys my age abducted from their homes in cities far from here and forced to sell drugs in a town they have never heard of, can barely pronounce the name of, and here you are. Giving me grief because you think I had something to do with a dead church going up in flames.

You seem very tense. Very angry.

— Well, aren't you Mr Observant. Yes, I'm angry. I'm angry that it's not safe to be young. I'm angry that people's identities can be weaponised against them. I'm fucking angry that this town is so burnt out.

Is that why you set fire to the church?

— Why this church? This broken house to spiders and ghosts only, with the smashed-in windowpanes and shattered brickwork. It's been empty my whole life. I've never felt a fucking thing towards it.

That's reason enough.

— I suppose, if I had done it. Some people want to see the world burn.

Are you quoting the Joker?

— When I was a little younger, maybe a year or two ago, I watched *Donnie Darko* for the first time. I love films. I'm like that child on the DVD cover of *Poltergeist*, with his hands on the TV screen. Anyway, I remember this scene, in the school classroom. I remember this scene so specifically because I remember having a crush on both Jake Gyllenhaal and Drew Barrymore. Ms Karen Pomeroy is quizzing the class on Graham Greene's short story, 'The Destructors'. In the story a group of teenagers torch an old man's house, the only house in the street to survive the Blitz.

I know the film. Are you suggesting that Old Misery is God, and the burning of his house is the burning of the church?

— Greene writes — which Donnie picks up on in the film — that destruction is another act of creation. I guess if the old man's house is now burned down, the whole street is on equal footing. They can build from the ground up, together. Start something new, with purpose, as a community.

Are you trying to say that you burnt down this church, as an act of creation, inspired by fiction?

— I'm saying that, whatever the circumstances, it was beautiful to see the community come together to share the experience.

Has it changed anything?

— We're just kids.

It's Black Country Out There

Fifty-five years since Aberfan. Fifty-five years since a black hole swallowed the entire town. Fifty-five years since black holes started to appear across Welsh towns and villages.

Some of them are small, or small to begin with. Easily missed, often human-sized; the circumference of a hula-hoop, or the wheel of a truck. Like the blue hole[1] on the bank of Colwyn Bay, where a small boy drowned on a family holiday in 2012. Or on the side of the cliff at Glyder Fach, Snowdonia, where a young man plummeted to his death in the middle of a storm in 1987, 1998, 2003, 2006, 2011.

2008: One woman, forty-eight, from Ystradgynlais, reported a black hole in the living room of her parents' house, where her father's chair used to be. She awoke one day and first thing, like every morning, rose to make tea. She put out three mugs, the kettle heating by a naked flame on the old-fashioned stove[2] and fitted the mugs with the teabags. Two sugars for her and Mum, one for Dad. It wasn't until the kettle shrieked that she remembered ah, yes, Dad died; Dad has been dead for three weeks now. She sunk into the sofa to have a think. As she gazed at her father's

---

[1] This is what they're called when they're underwater.
[2] She was living at her parents' house at the time, to help her mother look after her husband in his failing health.

empty chair, a black hole opened underneath it, and sucked the whole thing in.

***

The papers have gone through, I'll finally be moving in a month. I've been writing down my thoughts as they come to me, as my therapist suggested — about how I feel leaving the city, returning home — but the pages are scattered. I have a lot to say but there's plenty of research to get on with, and I've been so busy with my work. And Simon. It's been hard finding the time. Dad will be glad to have me back, in his way. I should have visited more, stuck around for longer after Mum died. The town isn't the same without her walking its streets, ever the flaneur. Coat pockets bulging with sweets and a camera roll full of snaps of church windows, empty tides, emptier shop fronts. It's still home, though, isn't it?

Well, I can start clearing out the flat. Decide what I'm going to keep of Simon's, his books, his clothes and camera equipment. Hire a van, say my goodbyes — that bit won't take long. I can't tell if this will be a fresh start, exactly, but it will be something different, something familiar. I am conflicted, yes. This flat has been a time capsule of my life with Simon, the years spent repairing our bicycles in the living room — I took the rug to the dump yesterday, it still had grease prints all over it — and our kitchen shelves capsizing with homemade ceramics, another one of Simon's short-lasting obsessions. I need the change. I have my paper to write, and I'll be in the right place to continue my research.

***

2013: A young family described the appearance of a black hole in their second bedroom. They'd recently moved into a small two-bed, terraced house in Neath to start a family after working hard and saving every penny for four years. Ethan, twenty-four at the time, ran his own company as a plumber, while fiancée Miya was a beautician. They considered themselves a normal couple who simply wanted to make a home. Tragedy struck them on 21 September, the end of summer, when their two-month-old baby, Sunny, died without cause. Just days after Sunny's passing, Miya says she was squeezed into the box room taken up by the chest of drawers and cot, cuddling the baby's soft toy bunny. That is when a black hole expanded across the floor. The cot was pulled in without a sound. Miya almost fell in — almost wishes she did, she says, a half-joke.[3] The couple reports the hole has never left, nor moved, in the years since. They've come to live with it.

***

It's surprising how much of your life you can fit in a van, the meat of it, the objects you've collected along the way that advertise the person you are. *Look at me!* my books seem to scream, *I'm a man of taste!* I'm aware of things underused, like the wok, and pointless, sentimental things, such as a paperweight in which the ashes of the old pup are cast in a suspended swirl. I guess it signifies the suspension of time in

---

[3] Maybe edit that bit out of the final draft. Not sure if suicidal comments, jokes or otherwise, are appreciated in academic papers.

grief, or something. Maybe I'm just the type of person to press my dead dog's ashes into a glorified marble. Simon loved that dog more than he loved me, I think. I don't know if I actually think that. It's all packed away now, in neat boxes.

The drive from London is mostly uneventful. The man I hired along with the van drives ahead, my little car following behind, boot sighing with its load. It feels a little gauche saying I've hired a man, but also, I quite like it. Simon would have found it funny. Somewhere between Cardiff and Bridgend, I watch a car drive straight into one of the black holes dotted along the M4. I drive slowly past Port Talbot to take in the sheer size of the hole between the town and the steelworks, and the grey sky sucking in the smog.

WELCOME TO LLANELLI, the sign reads, TWINNED WITH AGEN, FRANCE. When I google it later, that night, from the bed heaved up the stairs by me and the hired help, I read that Agen is a nice place to live. Situated on the River Garonne, between Bordeaux and Toulouse in Southwestern France, Agen is known for its brandied prunes, market gardens and Gothic architecture. While not exceptional, the city offers a pleasant quality of life with river walks and fairly cheap property prices. Sounds like a cruel joke, doesn't it? Being twinned with a town buried under the weight of its own past. Driving through Llanelli, it's as if the streets are closed to us; the muted palm slap of my heartbeat hitting every red light. The tedious drone of the car propelling towards somewhere neither I nor it want to be.

The street feels desolate when we arrive. There are no cars parked in the driveways of my new neighbourhood, quiet except for the gulls' crying in the face of the wind. The front wheel of the van dips into a pothole, about a metre wide, outside my new house. The driver mounts the curb next to the 'sold' sign pitched in the grass, and parks horizontally across my driveway. I feel a familiar distilling of anxiety in my blood, at the tilted axis of the parked van, fearing my furniture and possessions are either crushed or collapsed. On the other hand, it is gratifying to realise that I care so much about the possessions Simon left behind.

When we are both parked we stand around the pothole, which is in the road directly outside of my driveway. Standing around a hole like this with another man, hands in the pockets of our tight jeans, I feel charged. I kick a rogue pebble into the hole with my boot. The driver, scratching his chin, observes. His navy polo shirt is tight across his pecs, expressing the soft curvature of his nipples. The open collar of the shirt hints at a tanned neck, tightly coiled hair across the back of the neck and shoulders.

— You should complain to the council about that.

— Yeah.

— That's not right.

The driver never mentions any of the black holes we had to swerve around on the way here. So many! Some of them big enough to fit a whole bus.

The Pentre Nicklaus housing development in Machynys is comprised of houses that look 3D-printed. Perfect carbon copies with perfect white doors and sills, white guttering and white porches and white walls. Although, some of them have differently painted front doors, to give the illusion of the homeowner's individualism. Not bad for what was once described as a 'violent gypsy camp', a desolate wasteland mostly used for burning stolen cars. I've read all the *Wales Online* articles. Obviously they are *Wales Online* articles because they use the word 'gypsy' instead of 'traveller'.

It's one of the most successful[4] housing developments in Wales. Looking at the row of houses on my street, I see why it's called a housing *development*, not a housing *estate*. Same idea, different connotations. Most houses here, according to the estate agent[5], are sold to English second-homeowners — which is why, in this bleak mid-February, it's a ghost neighbourhood. Most of the people who can afford to buy houses here are retirees, happy to pay thousands for a view of the Gower and Carmarthenshire coast. Houses a Llanelli local cannot afford.

I take my bag and my box of research papers from the passenger seat and, one-handed, open the white door of my new home, with the key left for me in the pot of the artificial plant on the porch. I step, tentatively, into the living room; an empty, oblong vessel waiting to be filled. I am reminded of playing *The Sims* as a spotty, reclusive teenager, the only time I ever felt close to God. As I walk across the carpet and onto the kitchen laminate, I vaguely question whether I should take my shoes off. Simon would be tutting if I didn't take my shoes off. I keep them on — not because I want to defy him, but because I need to make this house my own. I like a dirty carpet, anyway — like crumbs on a kitchen worktop, it shows that a house holds life. My childhood home, there was a chest for

---

[4] See: desirable.
[5] Estate agent? Housing development agent?

shoes under the stairs and 'display' towels that were never to be touched. No dishes in the sink, no crumbs, new cushions every six months. It was like living in a showroom.

The master bedroom is without a view of the sea. Not that I requested a view, or could afford one of the houses that boast a view of the coast. I'm disappointed all the same. I sigh, just to fill the room's static, and place the box and my backpack on the floor, underneath the window, before going downstairs to relieve the van driver from singlehandedly dragging the back end of the desk over the pavement.

***

2005: The Machynys Peninsula Golf Club and Premier Spa opened, designed by Nicklaus and boasting a first-class golfing experience for beginners and professional golfers alike. Despite its success, hosting fourteen Championships — of which four were Ryder Cups — a mishap threatened to become a PR disaster for the newly opened health and sport centre, when local man, Pete Tomkins, was struck in the side of the head by a rogue golf ball. In the days following the accident, a black hole opened where family members had left bouquets of flowers.[6] Not all black holes are linked to an individual. Courthouses and jobcentres, for example, are riddled with them, all over the country. The same for hospitals, churches.

1993: I remember singing Christmas carols at Capel Als as a small boy, a black hole in place of the pulpit. One of the other boys kept leaning over the balcony, pretending to lose his

---

[6] It never made the news.

balance and fall in, for laughs. Ceased laughing when Miss Preece, a widow whose whole body was shaped like a pointed finger, got right up to his ear and whispered something that stopped him cold.

These are places teetering on the edge. At AA groups up and down the country there are more holes than chairs. Every drinking room is a crypt, their black holes barely visible through the carpet stains. I've spent too many afternoons in the backroom of my father's rugby club, at a sticky table with a book and an orange juice; the air thick with smoke and old alcohol, waiting for him to take me home to my mother.[7]

***

I've been in the house a couple of months now, absorbing the quiet, trying to fill it, writing letters to the council about the pothole— growing larger with each passing night. The fucking thing is halfway up my driveway. The other day, whenever it was, I — Christ, when was it? Last week? — I threw the paperweight containing our dead dog's ashes into the hole to test the deepness of its dark well. I never heard a break, never witnessed a whisper of smoke as the ash was released upon the explosion of its glass prison. Maybe the paperweight is still travelling through an infinite night. As it gets bigger and nearer, I want to seal it with all my possessions. All my books, the bed, the sofa, all my clothes, fucking everything. But what would I have left? An empty home, empty body.

I went for a walk in the town today. I've been avoiding the

---

[7] Too many personal anecdotes?

centre as much as possible. The *Llanelli Star* has offered me a few gigs as writer and photographer; talent shows, new store openings (not many of those) and fires (plenty of those). A bit of an income while I work on my paper. This morning I couldn't concentrate; I felt particularly moody because I found out that the 'pruneaux d'Agen', the famous Agen prunes, aren't produced in Agen but nearby villages, while the city handles distribution. It totally derailed my research for the day.

I needed to clear my mind, so I drove into town and parked at the multi-storey car park on Murray Street. I feel uneasy in the cold damp of this car park. Drivers intending to use the car park must first slowly skirt their car around the black hole on the slump leading up to the entrance, where a friend from my school years, after he jumped off the roof, had crumpled into himself.

Nothing's changed in the town: I already knew which churches are missing panes of glass, where pigeons make nests in the graffitied walls and crumbling plaster, and which shops are closed down, their windows smothered with posters for the circus that never seems to move on to the next ghost town. Towns like Llanelli are more black holes than pavement, like the acne of my pubescent years. The years I spent waiting to get away. I see my ugliness, both past and present, in every window of this town, and I remember why I left in the first place.

I brought my camera to document the size, scope and placement of each black hole, for my research. I approach one hole at random, on the floor in front of a cash machine on Stepney Street. I wish I could place my hand in it, find out its temperature, its texture. Would the hairs off my hand come out flat and damp against my skin, like I've plunged it into a pool of Stygian water? I don't know if they have a gravitational pull. I don't want to find out, so I keep a small distance.

Behind every abandoned shopfront is a black hole. And in every reflection, a version of me.

*　*　*

After brutal rounds of redundancies in the last decade across its steelmaking sites in Port Talbot, Caerphilly, Llanwern, Newport, Llanelli, Tata Steel is facing an even greater risk to its business than recessions, overseas competition and the decline of steel: the collective anger and despair of its laid-off workforce feeding into a black hole, one that keeps growing. Steel, once the making of Port Talbot, is now the breaking of it. The hole at the Port Talbot branch of Tata Steel is the biggest, with the factory and the town playing tug-of-war from separate sides.[8]

*　*　*

Why Aberfan?

Why didn't black holes crop up across the country after Senghennydd, or after an estimated fifteen thousand Welsh soldiers were killed during WWII, and almost a thousand children lost their lives in air raids?

---

[8] What do you do when they're killing themselves, but are completely dependent on each other?

What about the loss of Welsh language; the forced removal due to English sovereignty, Henry VIII's Act of Union in 1536; or phases of immigration to North America, Australia and beyond; the emigration of English language speakers to Wales during the Industrial Revolution; the forty thousand Welsh people at home during WWII who didn't speak English, who had only twenty minutes of Welsh broadcasted by the BBC per day, who felt this was England's war, not theirs?

In 1993, the Welsh Language Bill gave Welsh the same equal status as English, yet we, the Welsh, still continue to fight for its dignity, the respect our language deserves. Our history.

What about our grief, our anger?

Why isn't there a black hole for every lost community? For Blwych y Gwynt, Machynys, Brynmefys — these are just in Llanelli. Capel Celyn, the forced eviction of an entire village and flooded to create a freshwater reserve for Liverpool in 1965; Llanwddyn, flooded in 1888 to also create a reservoir for Liverpool; Temperance Town (destroyed in the 1930s to build a bus station), Newtown and Tiger Bay just three of the lost districts of Cardiff.

Why are there not black holes the size of a village for every lost or abandoned community?[9]

***

---

[9] Does it matter?

In all our years spent together, I never brought Simon here. Llanelli. I didn't want him to see this side of me, the place I'm from. When I dream of him — I still do — we're at opposite ends of a seesaw, legs dangling over a chasm of the blackest black. The hole absorbs all light. We can't see each other, but we can feel the other's weight at either end, us both responsible for the other's wellness, and their demise. I wake up most nights in a sweat, just as Simon begins to fall. The sudden lack of weight on his end of the saw slams me into the ground.

The stillness of the street is suffocating and sticky. I long for movement, a car, a pair of muddy walking boots left on the doorstep, but every house on this street is a mask hiding its darkness, empty rooms. The streetlights are matchsticks, burning out and bent over with the burden of their task, dispelling the heavy night until morning comes.

I stand at the open window and allow the night air to cool my damp skin. I read Simon's letter, the one he wrote before he left, the one he wrote before he lied about why we were breaking up — that he simply felt the relationship had come to its natural end. He didn't tell me he was ill. We shared everything, confided in each other — maybe that's why he couldn't tell me. The alarm clock by the side of the bed reads 2.37am. It is one year since Simon died from an illness that left him thin and weak and alone in an unknown hospital. When I think of him in the days leading up to his death, his stomach caved in and his eye sockets like two Magic 8 balls — give it a rattle; *Yes, No, Possibly, Maybe so, Ask again later.*[10] I think of how still he must have laid in that hospital bed, in practice for an eternity underground.

---

[10] What was the question again?

I look out the window at the street below. The pothole at night is a vacuum inhaling all colour. I watch it creep up the path and I wish it to swallow me whole. I wish for every black hole in this country to grow in size until there is no hill or stone or spruce tree left untouched. No railway lines, no factories, no waiting rooms, no churches. The coast behind the houses, the swampland and the peninsula, are all part of the black country landscape. This is a grieving country of which I am part of. This house means nothing to me. Why would it? This place never knew us, never knew Simon. Without him, I am in waiting. The hole has reached the front door.

Johnny Radio

Johnny croaks into an upright position in bed when he realises his radio is not in its usual place on the bedside table.

In the mornings his ears tune in long before his eyes blink open. He likes to enter the day with the jazz he used to dance to as a younger man. There are all the usual sounds — the birds, singing from the tree at the front of the house, cars revving up the hill. Spoons and bowls, cupboard doors. There are all the usual morning sounds — but no radio.

His back is stiff in the mornings, for what seems like many years now. Had he rubbed in his back cream the night before? Where the bloody hell is that radio! He manoeuvres himself to the edge of the bed, knees wobbling. His feet are numb to the cold, hard floor. He hacks up phlegm and spits it through the gap where a front tooth should be, into a glass dirty with dried spit on the bedside table. He eases into his slippers. Fluffy dragons look up at him from his feet. One of them is missing an eye.

Johnny usually goes to sleep listening to Jazz FM, so that he'll wake up with Alice Coltrane, Pharaoh Sanders, Ornette Coleman. Some of his and Anna's favourites. He kept listening, after she died, to keep her close. Sometimes in the middle of the night he wakes up to smoke in his chair by the window, and there will be music playing on Jazz FM's late-night mix. It will be whatever is popular — skinny young men with London accents, and rapping! Hardly sounds like jazz at all, to his ears. When he smokes, or when he can't sleep, he'll listen to late-night crime dramas, usually on BBC Radio Wales, with titles like *The Tragic Life and Death of Timothy Evan* then switch it back to the jazz station before falling asleep. Some mornings he'll wake up and the wrong programme will be playing, because he's forgotten to switch it back to the right channel, and he'll be in a grump for the rest of the day. The radio had been on the bedside table when Johnny fell asleep, that is where it always is when he goes to bed. For as long as Johnny can remember, there has always been a radio nearby.

He was just a boy when his father was bombed at the ordnance factory in Pembrey. He could no longer work. Johnny's mother washed clothes and bedsheets for the neighbours for money. Johnny, a big lad for his age, would help his sisters mangle the washing dry. The old wooden radio would broadcast reports on the war between Judy Garland and Bing Crosby's croons. They were ordered quiet when Frank Sinatra was on, his dad's favourite. His dad would be lying on the sofa with his leg elevated and his eyes closed, nodding along to 'I'll Never Smile Again'.

That dusty wooden radio lived on the windowsill, far enough from the dolly tub so that it wouldn't get wet or knocked into the water by a rogue elbow. Sometime in the fifties (Johnny can't remember when anymore) the dolly was replaced with a twin tub. The radio remained, only moved so the windowsill could be dusted by one of his sisters once a week. The radio never left the kitchen, but it would play loud enough that it could be heard from the living room. His father never left the sofa, all those years. He sat there and ordered everyone be quiet when his favourite jazz standards warbled through the living room from the kitchen, and he would nod along.

Johnny slowly stretches his arms above his head, groaning as his bones creak with the movements. The threadbare tracksuit bottoms he wears as pyjamas are inches too short. 'Ankle bashers', his grandchildren call them, the nasty little prats. The stretch of dirty yellow skin from the top of the slippers to the bottom of the trousers is mottled with splotches of blue, underneath patches of grey hair. The mess of purple veins scatter across his shins and ankles like map lines, feet that never left Wales.

The radio isn't anywhere around the chair either. The chair used to sit near the fireplace in the living room, in front of the TV. The first thing Rhian did when she and the children moved in after Anna died was to move the chair up to Johnny's bedroom. He tried to protest but she wouldn't have any of it. So here he sits, most of the day, opposite the window. The morning light fades through the window netting. The chair's upholstery is in rags; the cat's scratching post. Where is that little shit? If only she could talk and tell me where that damned radio has gone! He picks up his stick and lowers himself into the chair. The chair doesn't make a noise, the springs removed long ago after they wore through the fabric. Rhian had begged him to let her get rid of it, let her buy him a new chair. Mam wouldn't be mad at you for getting rid of it, she signed to him.

Johnny sweeps his stick under the bed, extracting a

number of socks, cat hair, fluff and cigarette butts; a handful of batteries rolling around on the wooden floor. Johnny catches a whiff of cat piss as he pulls out yellow copies of the *Llanelli Star* from under the bed. No radio. He sweeps under the bed one last time and hits something that yowls and hits back. Johnny feels a weight on the end of the stick and pulls it from under the bed. Twpsyn, hanging on to the stick with her claws and growling. Her off-white, ragtag old fur is nestled with dust. An old cigarette butt has embedded itself into the fur below her chin. Johnny tries to yank his stick back off her. She digs her yellow claws into the hazel. He can feel himself getting red in the face, can feel himself growing tired.

The stick slips from Johnny's hands and clatters to the floor. Twpsyn jumps onto Johnny's bed and begins to lick her paws, glaring at him from under her brow. He sits back in the chair for a moment and catches his breath. Maybe the radio is in the kitchen? Rhian or the kids might have seen it, at least. Johnny leaves the stick on the floor. The cat watches him as he shuffles towards the door then out onto the landing. The slippers make a scratching sound as they rub against the wooden floor. Twpsyn jumps down from the bed and sharpens her claws on the chair fabric.

Johnny grips the banister as he gingerly makes his way down the stairs. As he passes all the framed family photographs along the wall, the sound of spoons against cereal bowls gets louder. He can hear Rhian telling the children to hurry up or they'll be late for school. One of Johnny's slippers loses its grip and he falls down a step, knocking a photograph tumbling down the steps. It lands on the floor with a crash.

The photo was taken in front of a backdrop at a studio in town. The grandchildren are younger then, shards of glass where missing milk teeth should be. Their hair is fairer in the photo. They were both so blonde then. James sits on Rhian's lap in a sky-blue shirt, the collar artfully unbuttoned at the neck. Ella has her arms around Steve's neck. She has a bow in her hair and is wearing a gingham dress, like the one she wore to school when she was little. The gel in Steve's hair reflecting the photographer's studio light. Rhian and Steve are holding hands. And there's Johnny behind them, in a Scarlets rugby shirt. In the photo he is holding Twpsyn, then just a kitten. Smashed glass obscures their faces.

— Ohh, Dad, what have you done now? Rhian had rushed around the corner from the kitchen and now stands at the bottom of the stairs.

— It was an accident. Have you seen my radio? He signs back.

She retreats around the corner into the kitchen, reappearing at the bottom of the stairs with a dustpan and brush. Johnny leans against the wall on the bottom step while Rhian brushes all the little shards of glass into the pan. She's in her work clothes — black ballet pumps and skin-coloured tights, a black knee-length skirt and a plain blue blouse. Johnny doesn't know if she's happy. Probably too late for that. Rhian carefully picks the photo out of the broken frame.

— That's a shame, I loved that photo. She sighs, looking at her dead husband's forever smile. Are you alright? Have you had hurt?

Johnny shakes his head. His slipper had fallen off when he fell down the step and lies sole up. Rhian picks it up between finger and thumb and he silently lifts his foot in the air, for her to place it into the slipper for him.

He follows her into the kitchen. James and Ella are bickering at the table between mouthfuls. They fall silent when Johnny enters the room behind their mother.

— What are you fighting about now? Rhian asks them, an accusatory tone in her voice.

— James flicked his milk at me! Ella says, jabbing a finger at James.

— Can you stop acting a knob for two minutes? James says.

Ella reaches over and whacks him on the knuckles with her spoon.

— Ouch! Mam, tell her to stop!

The kettle is already full of water. Johnny flicks the switch and reaches over to take his mug from the dish rack next to the sink.

— James! Stop calling your sister a knob. And Ella, stop hitting your brother, will you? Can you please get to school now?

They both huff and drag themselves off their chairs. Johnny signs to them to ask if they've seen his radio but they don't notice, or maybe they're ignoring him. Johnny taps Rhian on the shoulder so that she looks at him, then he points to his mouth and then to the kids.

— Oi! Grampa is trying to talk to you! They turn to look at him.

— Have either of you seen my radio? Johnny signs at them. They shrug and shake their heads. Ella unlocks the front door. There's a brief moment of cars going past and children laughing at an unheard joke, before she leaves without saying goodbye. James says goodbye to his mam and wishes his grampa a good day. Before he reaches the front door, Rhian shouts after him:

— James! Your lunch! Johnny knows he is stalling for Ella to reach the end of the street with her friends before he follows her to school. James walks back into the kitchen and thanks her, making a big deal of kissing her on the cheek, then leaves too.

Rhian pours Johnny his coffee. He turns to her and waves his hand to catch her attention. When she looks at him, he signs:

— I can't find my radio. Have you seen it?

Rhian adds two heaped spoonfuls of sugar to her coffee, hesitantly swirls the spoon around the inside of the mug. The clatter of metal against ceramic punctuates the silence.

— No? Is it not on your bedside table, Dad?

— It wasn't there when I woke up. I don't know where it is.

Johnny sinks into a chair at the table. He feels like a wrinkled balloon. He grips the coffee cup with both hands. If Anna was still alive, she would know where to find the radio. She always knew where to find *things*. She never had a problem remembering things. Johnny searches the table for answers, its valleys of scratches. The old pine table is as much a part of the house as the walls themselves, but the kitchen is new. An extension of the house on Rhian's request. That must have been about... about eight years ago — or nine? Ten? Anna would have remembered; she always did.

— I'm sorry, Dad, I have to be off for work in a minute. There's leftovers from last night for lunch, okay? Are you going to be okay on your own?

He nods. He prefers being alone, having the house to himself. Rhian comes around the table and kisses him on the cheek, says she'll see him tonight and she'll make him something nice for his dinner. After the door bangs shut Johnny hears her locking it behind her.

Johnny wipes his damp chin with the back of his hand. The house is too quiet. Usually he would carry the radio down with him from his bedroom to the kitchen and he'd place it on the counter next to the kettle. He would sit at the table like he is now, with his coffee warming his hands, in his seat everyone knew not to sit in, and he'd listen to the local news. He loved hearing what was happening in the town, and there is never a dull moment. Some of his most memorable stories include a brawl in the Half Moon on New Year's Eve one year, a new fireworks shop opening in town, a young writer from the area had received a book deal, a few kids had been arrested in relation to the Park Church Fire. All interspersed with pop songs.

He grabs onto the sides of the table, purple fingers becoming translucent as he pushes his aching frame onto his feet. Where the bloody hell is that... is that... What was I looking for? Where the hell is my stick? Holding onto the walls for support, Johnny hobbles through the kitchen into the living room, which is permanently in a process of redecoration. Rhian changes the colour scheme along with the seasons. She is in the middle of switching from orange and grey to yellow and blue. The rug has that new smell. Johnny has the nagging suspicion that his pension is being spent on new cushions and Yankee candles and wooden slogans hanging from the walls: THIS IS A HOME, NOT A HOUSE and

COLLECT MOMENTS, NOT THINGS. For someone who collects moments, she seems to collect a lot of things.

He was asleep on the sofa when Rhian came home from work last night. Asleep with his radio on his chest, and when Rhian woke him up, he had struggled to catch his breath. She took the radio off his chest and placed it on the coffee table, told him he needs to be more careful. He'd awoken from a dream of a forest of broadcast towers. Johnny remembers the radio presenter was giving a report on some pop singer charged with — what was it? Murder? No, was it paedophilia?

Johnny sits down on the sofa in front of the blank TV, lost in thought. They'd had their dinner on their laps. Rhian cooked steak pie and mashed potatoes. Rhian asked Johnny to turn the radio off so they could watch TV, which he resented. He tucked the radio in between his leg and the armrest, and barely paid attention to the show on the screen. What was it? Some show where you watch people watch TV. Fucking stupid idea. He hates TV.

His parents couldn't afford a TV when he was growing up. His father had passed away, peacefully, on the couch. Johnny was stuck, working the fruit stall in the market, unable to leave home. By then all the houses on the street had their own washing machines, so his mother worked as a cleaner in the offices where Johnny's sisters answered phones. Every week, Johnny would keep back a small part of his pay and, after a few months of saving, which was easy to do after all his friends had moved to Port Talbot to try their luck at the steelworks, he treated his mum to a brand-new Bush radio, moulded from Bakelite plastic. It was brown and bulky with a large red face that lit up when the days got dark. It was ugly, but it worked. Everyone else on the street still had heavy wooden radios; some of them stood on the floor and were as large as a grandfather clock. Johnny's mother placed it in the front window, between the glass and the net curtain, for the whole street to see.

Johnny fell in love with Anna at a dance. They grew up on separate sides of the town — she was different from the girls he went to school with. She had strong calves, good for dancing and she listened to jazz like it was birdsong, the River Lleidi, wind. She listened like music was something that sweetened the taste of air.

She could dance even after everyone else was ready for home. Johnny would take her back to his mother's house, find a crooner or a country ballad they could slow dance to. On his mother's deathbed, Johnny promised he would never turn the radio off.

That brown Bakelite radio had broken down at the wake after Anna's funeral, years later. Rhian's children were barely out of nappies then, too young to remember. Steve was still alive too, immensely proud of his young new family, and patient with Rhian's father. In those days Johnny could speak still, and did so in short, clipped utterances. He was a man of few words even then. Under his black blazer he wore a red Scarlets tie that Anna had bought him as a thirtieth anniversary present, neatly fastened with a silver tie clip engraved with *John and Anna Parker, Married 5th June 1970*. He wore the tie and clip at every given opportunity. Anna was very sick when she died. She lived longer than anyone thought she would, as if to prove them all wrong.

The day of the funeral was tough on Johnny. Rhian had wanted to turn the TV on when everyone went back to the house afterwards for cans of Guinness, triangles of sandwiches and mini sausage rolls. Fucking TV, at a wake? Johnny had hissed at her; your mother would be turning in her bloody grave! Rhian had suggested putting the TV on to some music channel to stop Johnny from banging on the Bush radio on the windowsill. Over the years it had been opened up and its insides messed around with, parts replaced and rewired, but it had never failed, until now. It was as much a member of the family as all the cats Johnny had growing up. Rhian sighed and walked the rounds among the guests. Johnny kept banging on the side of the radio and muttering under his breath. It buzzed with static and fluttered between warbles of noises. Johnny brought the bottom of his fist down hard on the radio's head and then, suddenly. That song. *Their* song.

Before she could push her way through the crowded kitchen to stop him, Rhian saw Johnny wrenching the plug out of the socket, and push through the bodies of black suits and black dresses to the patio doors with the radio under his arm. He opened the door and threw it into the garden. It crashed onto the stones, metal shrapnel and chips of brown plastic shattering into the weeds lining the wall. There it lay face up, looking up at the overhanging branches of the crab apple tree, surrounded by its guts and bolts.

Johnny looks at the pictures of his mother and Anna on the mantlepiece and lets out a long, deep sigh. Their eyes are watching him. The radio isn't here, he can tell. His bones are too weak to pull the room apart to look for it, anyway. He struggles to his feet and limps over to the patio doors. Johnny opens the door and steps out into the garden. The old Bakelite radio is sitting outside next to the door, the one he smashed all those years ago. Johnny got so adamant that the radio was to not be thrown out that he became hysterical.

Some years later, when Ella was old enough to explore and question everything she saw, she managed to pull down the ladder that leads into the loft, using Johnny's stick. She found the radio in a corner covered in a thick film of dust and spiders' webs, and brought it down. By then Johnny had stopped talking, just woke up one day without a voice. He wrote for Ella, the radio was once a gift he gave his mother, who then gifted it back to him when she died. He told Ella, Johnny and her grandmother Anna grew fond of each other over their shared love for the jazz channel and old radio dramas. Ella took the beat-up radio into school the next day, and when she brought it home, it had been cleaned inside and out, the casing put together and a hole cut in the top. She told Johnny she'd planted seeds inside it. They can water the seeds together, and turn the radio into something alive and beautiful again. How did he feel? Why can't he remember?

Johnny coughs up phlegm from deep in his lungs and spits it through the gap in his front teeth. Twpsyn appears from the hedge lining the garden wall, and grazes against his bare ankle. Johnny thinks he hears music from over the garden wall, the chorus instantly recognisable through all the sounds and songs in the world. He's transported to that day. Their friends and family looking on with love, mothers choking back tears. Anna was beautiful, so beautiful. She wasn't a delicate woman, but he handled her with care, following the steps he had practised, rehearsed in secret. They follow each other around the dance floor of the rugby club, their eyes for each other only. Everyone else fades to black and it's just them, twisting in the dark. The song cuts to an advert for Machynys Golf Club, and Johnny wonders where the hell his radio could be. Anna would know. She would find it in a heartbeat.

Ten reasons why I didn't stop Danny Jenkins from throwing your brother into a bin:

1   It all happened very quickly.
2   I thought someone else would stop Danny Jenkins. This was naïve of me. No one ever did. The nature of the bystander — an inability to take control or responsibility when part of a crowd.
3   I have an empathy score of 7/80. No, really. I didn't know this at the time — I was simply known as a miserable git. *Dead inside,* everyone said. I have come to learn that I have trouble processing my own emotions and identifying the emotional state of others in the moment. There's a great divide between my concept of emotion and my acknowledgement of it. Alexithymia — it's linked to my autism. I didn't 'feel' like your brother was in any distress.
4   Maybe my lack of empathy for his position, as the one being thrown in the bin and not the thrower, comes from a place of privilege. I have never been thrown into a bin, at school or otherwise. I couldn't empathise with your brother.
5   It was quite funny.[11]
6   Danny Jenkins was a brute. He was as happy slinging

---

[11] What could I have done, anyway?

hooks as he was pushing people to buy chocolate bars out of his backpack.

7   Danny Jenkins sold me chocolate bars and energy drinks my mother didn't let me have at home.

8   One's silence is another's source of strength. I inadvertently gave Danny Jenkins the strength to throw your brother into a bin on school grounds. I wish I could say my silence was out of empathy for your brother, an offering of comfort, but it wasn't. This is more of an apology than a reason.

9   We were in Year 9. Your brother was in Year 8. This was the natural order of things — the food chain of the school years. Which is why, when you came to rescue your brother, we backed down. Even Danny Jenkins. You were a Year 10.

10 It was raining and I wanted to go home.

Who Are You Calling Kim Woodburn?

No one calls me Kim Woodburn to my face. No one would even fucking try.

One time, at the café I own opposite the train station, on the corner of Glanmore Street and Western Crescent, a man called me, not just Kim Woodburn, but a waxwork model of her, like the ones at Madame Tussauds, only half-melted. I poured disinfectant into his tea when he wasn't looking. No one stopped me. No one batted an eye. Even my ex-husband knows not to take the piss with me.

The café looks out onto a children's nursery, a taxi rank and the railway lines. Here, I will be honest with you — the interior is drab, its décor outdated; plastic everything in shades of brown and green. The legs of the tables rock back and forth. It's like eating your dinner off a seesaw. The tables get covered in ketchup and sugar and tea rings and pools of vinegar throughout the day. The men who come in here eat like animals. On the windowsill next to the door is a stand holding brochures for Folly Farm, Oakwood, Ffwrnes Theatre, the Wetlands Centre. Sometimes people fold a brochure to place under a table leg to keep it steady. The more the table rocks, the more times they fold the brochure. On the way out they unfold it and try to rub the creases out, before returning it to the brochure stand. They wouldn't want to piss me off.

No matter how hard they stamp on the mat, the green lino

floor is sticky from years of workmen's boots bringing dust in. Sometimes they stamp their boots on the way out too. Years and years of grease and oil and mopping. The regulars know not to scrape their chairs back against the floor. I've been known to lob a teaspoon at someone's head. The coffee machine and the fryer are so loud I am yelling every day, all the time. My throat is raspy like the bottom of an old pan from years of it — that and smoking. The chairs are cockroaches that look like they survived doomsday, spindly metal legs and the vinyl skin cracked and peeling. Some of them, their yellowing cushion foam pools out like a leaking spot. I'd replace every chair if I could, if I had the money. I would replace everything. But this is my kingdom. Do not complain.

If anyone was to ask, my proudest achievement is the score on the door: a perfect five. The black-and-green sticker is the first thing someone sees before they step across the threshold. Not that many customers look at it; mostly builders, tradesmen and taxi drivers in need of a hot, quick breakfast. The state of their trousers — they don't care how clean a kitchen is. There's a certificate in pride of place next to the piece-of-shit coffee machine. That had been a gift from my mother, when the café was recently opened, when Mum was still alive. Electricity crackles when the plug is pushed into the socket. When it's in use something rattles, a loose screw perhaps. I often turn it on just to drown out the voice of someone I doesn't like. At night I lock up, and the sound of the coffee machine follows me home.

There are two girls who work for me. Maria speaks very little English but understands when spoken to her. She never works outside of the kitchen and leaves it only for a smoke break. She is quick, a good employee, and very thorough. She is clean too: her nails neat and short, her hair always tied back and in a net. One time someone found one of her hairs in their food, and she was inconsolable. She begged to keep her job; she has two young boys to feed. She drinks coffee like water. And scalding hot too, fresh from the machine. When she receives a burn or bad news she swears in Romanian and it is beautiful. The girl, Martyna, delivers hot plates of food to the table and flirts with the men. She's new and wears lipstick, her nails painted red or bubblegum pink. When a customer told Martyna I look like Kim Woodburn, she asked in a thick Polish accent: who is that? I liked that. Martyna is new, she has promise. She's yet to be broken in — there's nothing good that'll come from flirting with these sorts of men. They may flirt back, and some of them may be honest, but they won't be interested in the likes of her, a single mother with credit card debt.

The café is due an inspection any day now. Anyone who comes in who isn't wearing steel-capped boots and cargo trousers covered in paint or dust is suspicious. Every night at closing time I give my orders. Every night I bark like a dog at Maria and Martyna to do the jobs I can't. I am not young or thin anymore. Maria climbs the worktop to take down the air vent panels above the oven, while Martyna stands with her arms above her head, ready to grab the panels and place them in the sink full of soap and hot water. There's a tiny dishwasher that looks like it's stepped out of the seventies, as beige as the rest of the kitchen, including the walls and the ceiling light. In the years since the smoking ban you really notice the ceiling stains. This place and me, we have not aged well.

Maria and Martyna take everything out from the fridge and freezer, label and relabel fruit, veg, eggs, meat and milk by their use-by dates and throw out anything that has begun to turn. Then they take out the trays and wipe clean the insides with rags and anti-bacterial spray. They wrinkle their noses at the smell of watery blood that leaks from black puddings to the bottom of the fridge. They take out the bins and wipe down the worktops, microwave, kettle and toaster. The oven is rarely used but they clean it out regardless. They scrub the air vents that had been soaking in the sink. After they are washed, they are left on the side to dry, ready to be placed back over the oven in the morning. They drain the soot-black water and refill the sink with clean water and soap. The fryer baskets are dropped in the water to soak and the old oil drained from the commercial fryer, then filled with new oil, to be heated in the morning. While Maria and Martyna carry out their tasks, I count the money in the till, keep my paperwork in order, make sure the first aid kit under the counter is filled with the required supplies of gauze, tape and blue plasters. I know Maria and Martyna sneak food into their bags. Sausages that are turning, stale bread and overripe tomatoes. I never say anything. I know how it is.

The other day, when I was on the lookout for anyone who may be a Food & Hygiene Inspector, a tall man with broad shoulders walked in wearing black bootcut jeans and biker leather. He sat down facing the door, scraped the chair back and wiped the table with a leather forearm — strike one. He had a salt-and-pepper goatee, and the cut of his hair made his head look square. He ripped a brochure into squares and thrust them under a table leg, the bastard. Strike two. When I approached his table to take his order, he looked at me through sunglasses that were too small for his face. I couldn't see his eyes. He asked for a Desperate Dai breakfast and a black coffee with a voice cut with smoke. You never know who could be a snake in the grass but he didn't seem like the health inspector sort. When I brought him over his coffee, he looks me up and down over the top of his tiny sunglasses.

— Has anyone ever told you, you look like Kim Woodburn?

I swear to God, the whole café stands still. Everyone turns to face us, necks straining. A sliver of egg yolk stuck to someone's moustache plops onto their plate. Slices of fried bread soak up baked bean juice and become soggy. Forks full of bacon and egg white dangle mid-air between mouth and plate. This can go only one way, they must be thinking, she's going to batter him. They're about to be witnesses to a murder. No one will confess anything. They'll tell the police it was a freak accident. They saw nothing. He threw his own coffee in his own face.

— Who's you calling Kim Woodburn? I ask, all calm like.

— Didn't mean to offend, love, I'm a talent scout for an agency that manages celebrity impersonators. He holds his hands up like two white flags.

— Look at me, I'm Ron Pearlman from *Sons of Anarchy*. We have a cracking Noel Fielding, Alan Carr. 2009-era Lady Gaga. We also have a bloody good Theresa May, and a Margaret Thatcher who mostly lies in a coffin and pretends to be dead. You'd be a great Kim Woodburn. I know talent when I see it. Look, I'll leave you my card.

Some day after the Ron Pearlman incident — it could be two days, five days, a week; every day is the same — I am sitting at one of the sticky tables in the silence before I open the café. I sip a black coffee and nibble a piece of toast, when there is a thud at the front door. I look up from the *Radio Times* magazine I am flicking through to see a flash of red past the window, and an unassuming letter on the mat, a slip of white against the dusty brown. Mail is bad news. Bills and tax and junk. This letter is like the rest. Bad news. Except, this is worse! A perfect five has become a four. I read the letter over and over again. I choke down sobs, I don't cry. Dirty water in the mop bucket and left on top of a worktop. How could I have overlooked something so small?

When Maria arrives for work at 7am and Martyna a little later, I don't have the heart to berate them. When Martyna turns on the coffee machine and receives a small jolt of an electric shock, I don't even smile. Nothing can console me. The day goes by in a daze, customers come and go. When I turn off the lights and lock the doors, I know it will be for the last time. I am done. I wait at the railway line to cross and feel the cold barrage of air from the train whip around my face. The barriers lift and I walk through the empty streets, passing the Whitstable Inn, hollow laughter and a jukebox waltz. The noise of the coffee machine doesn't follow me home, not that night. I arrive home. I call out for the cat, stand by the back door rattling treats in the box, but he never comes. Maybe he is gone for good this time. I think this every night.

If someone asks, I tell them I'm fine. Fine, that's the word. When my last cat got ravaged by a fox, I was fine. Fine when I divorced Jimmy Pugh. Fine, with a pint and a pack of dry roasted nuts at the Whitstable after work. I am so lonely, but how can I admit it? I have reputation. I don't need anyone. But there are nights where I think of ending it all, when I feel my kingdom being pulled from me, like slipping on a freshly mopped floor without a caution sign. Like a four on the door instead of a perfect five. I have these thoughts when I am alone in bed, after another night of soaps and TV dinner. Another night of balancing the books and running a business. Nights where the cat won't answer my calls. Even the cat would rather be anywhere else. The tuna scraps taste better from a neighbour's hand. I don't think about ending my life in the literal sense. That was only once, when I stuck a fork in the dodgy socket the coffee machine is plugged into. I thought the electric shock would be strong enough to stop my heart, dead in a beat. But life goes on, one shitty coffee to the next. Even the coffee machine continues to plod onwards.

This night is one of those nights. I lie on top of the crisp white sheets of my king-sized bed, myself a lonesome vehicle, the bed's borders on either side stretching away into the distance like a highway, thinking about the way I thought it would end. This life. I always thought I'd go out on my own terms. Imagine, being brought down by a four out of five. I have a reputation! The whole town is going to laugh at me. What's the point?

I dream, when I dream, of setting the café on fire, making it look like an accident. I could collect the insurance money and move somewhere warm, like Majorca or Benidorm. Or I could sit among the flames and melt like a waxwork figure. Is spray tan flammable? I could become someone else. I should have given up the café years ago — I've barely kept up with the payments for years. And everything needs replacing. The only thing that has stopped me was Maria and Martyna. Both mothers, desperate, and deserving of kindness. They were, are, my girls. I need them as much as they need me, but I can't think about that. I need to become someone else. I need to become someone else.

I flip Ron Pearlman's card over in my sand-dune hands, dry and folded from years spent in sinks and bleach. I ring the number on the card. It rings three times before he picks up with a movie-star hello.

— It's me, from the café. I want to be your new Kim Woodburn.

That night I dreamt of a beach, each grain of sand a coin. It's night and I'm lit up by a helicopter's spotlight. I've got my hair pulled back in a bun so tightly I feel my skin tearing from my bones. There's a beach hut on fire. I turn to face it and it's the café. The windows explode silently, glass mixed with coins. I try to run towards it, I begin to sink. Maria and Martyna reach for me. I look to them, desperately; they are mops with marigold hands and ragdoll hair. They can't help me. My sand-dune hands crumble to nickel and copper.

Brief Interview with Condemned Child #3

Would you like to tell me why you started the fire?

— There is nothing I could say that will make you change your mind. You think we did it, that's fine.

Is that a confession?

— Do you know how I became friends with the others?

No, they haven't mentioned it.

— We became friends at a funeral. Really, that's where our friendship began. All three of us are in the same school year but never really hung out. Someone in our year died. No one knows how, exactly. He may have choked on his own vomit. He was someone all the girls fancied because he was tall and had an earring. He was an arsehole, but no one should die like that.

Like that?

— Alone.

Is this something you're anxious of? Being — and dying — alone?

— I follow the other two around because together we make a community. One of the things we do together, we walk around the town. We walk around the reservoir and watch the rain distort our reflections. We walk to the west side of the beach and watch the trains plummet the coast towards Pwll and Burry Port. We walk through the town centre and try to imagine it as it was when our parents were young, and the town was alive.

What else do you do on these walks, except watch?

— I was given a camera for Christmas. One of Mum's old film cameras from her collection. I take pictures of our reflections in the windows of vacant properties. Retail units with mannequins collecting dust in their outstretched hands, coat hangers on the floor like fish out of water. All the new retail spaces in East Gate, built out of hope and a promise they would regenerate the town. They're worn and decrepit before they've been used, given a purpose. The Travelodge, for whatever reason it was built, only services ghosts. The two businesses that actually get people through the door are Nando's and the tanning booth.

You sound quite judgemental of people who like a fake tan and Nando's chicken, and the connotations implied by these two things in relation to each other.

— Renovation and regeneration often rely on corporate self-aestheticisation. Expensive, Instagram-ready cocktails and fast fashion.

What does this have to do with the fire?

— Did you know arts and culture contributes £2.1 billion to the Welsh economy annually, and employs at least 50,000 people? Where is the culture in Llanelli? Why aren't all these empty retail units from East Gate to Opportunity Street to Station Road filled with artist studios, galleries, independent cinemas, bookshops, community workshop hubs? There's a new fireworks shop, great. How does that benefit anyone? What opportunities are there for people my age, what are we supposed to do for fun?

What about events like Llanelli Pride? That was a positive, impactful event for the community, and there were so many people there.

— Yes, and everything was sponsored by local law firms and dental practices.

How deep is your apathy?

— It's quite like a black hole.

If you were to commit a crime, how would you feel about it? Would you care?

— I believe my lack of enthusiasm for the present only doubles my effort in caring about the future. I care very much about building and contributing to a sustainable community, finding positive solutions. I care about the public ownership of railways and utilities, and the accessibility of opportunity for everyone.

Could the destruction of private property be considered a creative, positive force?

— It could certainly be considered that way.

You know, if you or your friends had anything to do with this fire, an apology would go a long way.

— Apologise for what? Like so many of the buildings around here, we are condemned.

A Congregation of Cygnets

William Williams was waiting for something interesting to happen.

He wore sensible clothes: black or navy-blue cord trousers and Oxford shirts in block colours, rusted orange or off-white. Sometimes, when feeling particularly contemplative, he wore a tweed blazer. He picked his outfit the night before and ironed it in the morning. Every Christmas he was given aftershave by an aunt, which he was careful to make last the whole year. In the morning he applied lip balm after brushing his teeth and moisturised every evening before going to bed. He was sullen at the breakfast table if he didn't get his full eight hours of sleep. After getting dressed in his freshly ironed outfit and tying his bootlaces tight, William checked the weather app on his phone to decide what coat would be most suitable for leaving the house. He was awaiting his A-Level results, which would determine if he'd go to the University of Bristol to study English. He wanted to move further away from home, somewhere like Glasgow or Norwich, but didn't want to upset his mam with the distance.

William had studied English at Coleg Sir Gâr Graig, alongside religious studies (with philosophy) and media, where he first discovered James Joyce's *A Portrait of the Artist as a Young Man*, Strindberg's *A Dream Play*, and how to write in metaphor. He found the Cartesian Dualism theories confusing but found comfort in Descartes' development of knowledge based on mathematical logic and reason. Descartes' theories aligned with his world view; he'd tell anyone who'd listen. During his breaks, William walked to the beach opposite the Graig to eat his lunch. The tide was usually out when he was there, revealing a barren landscape of flotsam: old ropes and rotten wood, beer bottles and crumpled bike frames. The sky was more often grey than not, as if it was offended by the proposal of even a little bit of sun.

During the summer William was awaiting his A-level results, he continued to walk slowly along the beach and sit on the rocks. Mr Matthews, who taught English at the Graig, said he had a good head for writing and encouraged him to write stories. When he presented Mr Matthews with his writing, Mr Matthews responded to it positively and said he should try to get them published. One afternoon William was particularly morose after receiving a rejection email from the editor of an online magazine he had sent a story to. He wore his tweed blazer to the beach and sat on a rock, gloomily eating an apple, and contemplated a printed copy of his rejected story. The story, it had been commented on, was pretentious drivel. It had referenced *The Rime of the Ancient Mariner*, the albatross hung around the neck of the young sailor. And wasn't it so transparent? That William saw himself as the sailor, adrift and burdened? After all, the final line read, 'For all he knew, he was the last human alive.'

William wasn't quite sure what his story had meant upon completion, but he thought he had something worthy of publication. He had been proud to be able to write with such abstract thought — he was so sure it would be published! But the editor said it was, 'without being harsh', a bit melodramatic. William saw this as teacher-talk for the story actually being quite shit. He threw the apple core in the direction of the sea, dissatisfied with the lack of a *thump* when it hit the sand. Folding the pages of his story and placing them back in the inside pocket of his blazer, William rose to his feet and started to meander through the rocks. When he was younger, he liked to skip from one rock to another. Sometimes the wind would carry his little frame too far forward and he'd catch a wrist or palm across the crags. He never minded, never cried out. He liked searching through the rocks, looking for rusted tins and car tyres, an Asda trolley covered in moss, its legs sticking in the air like an animal with rigor mortis.

The tide was still out, somewhere near the Gower. The sky hanging over the exposed seabed reminded him of the sky he'd written into his story: 'a vast field of space, a cemetery of clouds pressing down on his face like a damp cloth. The Lost Boy tried to open his mouth, to pull out a lyrical scream, a horrific orchestra, but the sky flooded his mouth, choked and burned him.' William walked across the rocks, down to the far end of the beach. He stopped for a moment and looked to his right, past the railway lines that stretch through Pwll, towards Burry Port and Carmarthen. In front of the breakwater — one half of a crab-like pincer — a boy threw a stick for two black dogs with sandy fur to chase. It spun defiantly in the lack of wind, and William felt jealous of the *thwack* it made on the hard sand.

He hated his name. Who names their son William Williams? He had resented his parents for it since he was in nursery, when the other kids, snotty noses and hands painted with felt-tip pens, called him Willy Willy. It remained with him throughout school. His teachers at St John Lloyd's Catholic Secondary School could hardly contain their smirks when ticking off the register and did little to put a stop to the incessant ribbing. The only time they used their authority was to punish William for throwing a rugby boot at Danny Jenkins' head in the boys' changing rooms. Danny had tried to push him, fully clothed, into the showers — a literal take on a 'Wet Willy'. Mr Mason had to step in before a fight broke out. The sort of fight where the pugilists are surrounded by boys with scruffy ties and oily skin. In that moment they would have been gamblers at an underground fight club, pushing each other for a better view. They cheered for their champion while the smallest (often the youngest of that academic year) stood on the benches, overcompensating for their lack in stature by cheering the loudest, hoping no one would hear their voices crack.

Mr Mason, the PE teacher at St John's, called William's parents to his office after the incident. William and his mother sat on the opposite side of Mr Mason's desk, his dad stood aggressively silent behind them with his arms folded, their backs to the door. Mr Mason sat upright in his swivel chair, in tracksuit bottoms and blue hoodie, nervously passing his whistle from hand to hand as he retold the events to William's parents. His mother avoided Mr Mason's eye when promising him her son would be grounded at home. The car journey home was silent, the air electric with tension that The Wave FM could not break.

— I never did trust a bloke with trainers as clean as that, see, William's father said, upon entering the family home on College Hill. Especially when worn by a PE teacher, mun.

— Ohhh don't be silly now, Evan, his mother replied. He's just trying to keep Will out of trouble, ain't he?

— Maybe, love, but has he called Danny Jenkins' parents in for a talk? I know his dad from the rugby club. Good prop back in the day, his dad was, not a nice sort though. Evan turned to his son, who was quietly unlacing his black school shoes.

— You haven't done anything wrong, boy, we only said we'd ground you to Mr Mason to keep him happy. He put his hand on William's shoulder. There will always be boys like Danny Jenkins.

When he ran out of rocks, William climbed up to the walkway that continued towards the café. The car park behind it was full, whole families sitting inside their vehicles with the windows down, seatbelts off and sweaty foreheads, sharing KFC buckets. The only car park bin was overflowing with fast food wrappers and ice lolly packaging. A mound of cigarette stubs, surrounded by tails of ash, exuded a sharp smell, like car fumes with vinegar, that made William feel nauseous when he walked past.

— You have a cracking name for writing, William Williams. A proper author's name, Mr Matthews had once said to him.

William didn't share his teacher's optimism, so all his notebooks, his pencil case, his essays, exams, poems and stories were monogrammed with *W. Williams*. Would the story have been published if I'd written my full name? he thought. He went to sit on a bench, next to an old man holding a Calippo in one hand, a triangle of a sandwich in the other, a copy of

The Sun balanced on his lap, to write a poem on his phone about the bin. It wasn't long until he gave up. The old man didn't look up nor speak to William and didn't seem to notice when the Calippo melted onto his knuckles.

William walked along the North Dock, crossed the roundabout onto Marine Street and went past the Bucket and Spade, its picnic benches empty. Outside slogans such as *Strongbow sold here!* were printed on banners. Further down the road Mr Chips claimed to sell the best chips in the town, and sold them out of a shop that was once a living room in a terraced house. The smell of vinegar followed William past the boarded-up Cambrian, the Felinfoel Ale dragon looking defeated on its battered sign, with no breeze to give it wings.

The barriers were down when William reached the train tracks. A row of cars either side waited impatiently, their windows lowered. Heavy bass banged out in basic rhythms; a lack of discernible melody persisted. Radio hosts presented the news and told drivers how hot it was, in case they hadn't realised. Cyclists, dazzling in high-vis, tapped at their smartwatches and swore under their breath. On the other side of the track, two shirtless men in paint-covered cargo trousers smoked outside the Carwyn James, half-empty pints on the step. They shouted over at someone they recognised on William's side of the track. Stressed by all the noise at the crossing, William closed his eyes, and counted his breaths. When the train roared past, he clicked his fingers and counted the seconds until it was no longer visible. As soon as the barriers were lifted the cyclists took off with a chorus of *Fucking finally!* William waited for all the cars and cyclists to ride past before he crossed the tracks himself.

*

William knew his parents felt partially to blame for his resentment of them. They had wanted to give him a strong Welsh name; he had come from a long line of strong Welsh names. His family held their nationality at the centre of their identity. William's grandfather Thomas had sung in a male choir at Capel Als on Marble Hall Road on Sundays, after serving in Singapore during the war. Afterwards the choir would soothe their throats with Felinfoel Double Dragon or Brains Dark, before going home to the roast dinner their wives prepared for them. Thomas Williams had black-and-white pictures of himself in dragon face paint at a Six Nations match on his mantlepiece, and he had the voice of a Celtic saint. The choir travelled the Commonwealth, singing in Welsh, but he always said his favourite song to sing was 'Hen Wlad Fy Nhadau'. William's parents had named him after James James, its composer. When William's father, Evan Williams, was drunk on a Friday afternoon, he told William he was named after Evan Evans Brewery. Maybe there was truth in both.

It was approaching late afternoon when a fire engine roared past. William covered his ears. Over the roofs of the shops and takeaways on Station Road, a trail of grey smog curled towards the sun. On William's left, Jimmy Pugh's fireworks shop, open only for three or four months a year, was separated from the rest of the street by shutters covered in faded graffiti, while Jimmy himself was often seen drinking Stella out of a chalice at the Halfway Hotel. Has the Oasis Café ever sold a single slice of toast? William wondered. Its boards had slogans and tags scratched into it where windows should be. A sign nailed into one of the boards said NO POSTERS! Underneath it, a poster for the Burry Port Carnival was Blu-Tacked on. Smashed bottles were strewn across the pavement outside the Windmill and Barnums, closed now, with paint peeling from their doorframes. The sound of glass being crushed into the ground as mothers pushed prams through the shards made William jump.

William remembered the old military cap, stuck through with enamel pins his grandfather Thomas had bought, of every country's flag he had visited with the choir. Up until his death, he was adamant it was Nana Williams' special gravy that allowed him to sing so beautifully. His own son, Evan, was proud to come from such a musical background. He learned piano at the Capel and was a good choir boy. He grew up in the Half Moon, played rugby for New Dock Stars, drank bitter from the age of sixteen and fell in love with a girl whose father owned a butcher's. William still had the hat, in a box somewhere at the bottom of his wardrobe. He had written a story about it once. Mr Matthews had said it was a cracking story. William inherited the hat after his grandfather died. Sometimes it felt like the town died with him.

Behind the carpet shop the Gallaghers used to own on the corner, past the Polish supermarket with neon lighting, Home Bargains, Home Start and Jaja Fashions with newspaper glued to the upstairs windows, a plume of grey smoke could be seen streaking upwards. Thick like flowing water, a different grey to the sky. At the top of Station Road cars from three directions rumbled like metal woodlice. More fire engines waiting at the red lights. On one side, the Old Theatre Elli, not proud of its listed status, was an architectural eyesore. Brown brick and yellow-grey tiles were dubiously protected by construction scaffold and metal fences. No work had been done on its exterior for as long as William could remember. It hadn't even been graffitied or vandalised; too depressing. On the opposite corner, the staff of the Vista Lounge stood on the street with no patrons to care for, all three of them in black button-down shirts with the sleeves rolled up past their elbows, looking up at the blackening sky.

William would visit his grandfather Thomas with his father, in the care home he was put in up until his death. He would listen to them criticise Nia Griffith's efforts to tackle climate change and what she was going to do with all the empty churches, all the empty shops on the high street. They debated the headlines in the *Llanelli Star*, called it a rag of a paper — something William partially agreed with. In truth, he didn't think it was as bad as they made out, but he had been embarrassed to show his face at their office, on the corner of Cowell Street and John Street, since he trod dog shit into their office carpet on his first day of work experience earlier that summer.

William crossed the road to turn right onto Murray Street with his fingers jammed in his ears. A police car rounded the corner, siren blaring, into the street. Two policemen were cordoning off the road after the police car passed and shouted at any cars who tried to follow, regardless of the crowds of people and emergency vehicles. As he neared, William saw the church was on fire. The Congregational Park Church, on the corner of Murray Street and Inkerman Street. Young children sat on their father's shoulders, watching firemen unrolling their hoses.

The air, already choked from the warmth of the day, was hotter still from the fire. The smell of burning wood and decades of dust coated William's tongue with an acrid taste. A tile fell from the burning roof and a policeman shouted,

— Get back!

Nobody listened, the policeman didn't care. This was the most excitement he'd had since confiscating alcohol and weed from the unofficial Year 11 post-prom beach party. William had gone because his only friend, Emma Lee, had gone, and he didn't want her to think he was, in her words, a *pussy*. He recognised the policeman from that night by his shirt unfastened three buttons too low, exposing a chest devoid of hair, and perfectly fake-tanned. He chewed gum with his mouth open, his eyes darting for an excuse to tell someone off. The policemen either side of him hardened their eyes as if to stop them involuntarily rolling whenever he spoke.

Stained glass flecked the pavement in hues of dusty green and wine red. Jesus was in bits, pieces of him crushed underfoot or in the bushes between the cast-iron railing and the black stone of the church, its face gaunt and hollow. Flames raged behind the empty holes where its glass eyes should be. Johnny Radio, head to toe in official Scarlets merchandise, shuffled through the crowd, his digital radio under his arm. He elbowed his way to where William stood watching, listening to The Wave's hosts report on the fire while watching the flame's theatrics in front of him. With the other hand shaking hesitantly, as if trying to remember the mechanism of shaking, he tried to light a king-sized cigarette. The flint had gone in the lighter. He nudged William and motioned for a light. William shook his head and watched him shuffle through the crowd. He caught a fragment of a pop song, something about not being able to start a fire without a spark — surely not? — on Johnny's radio, before the policeman started shouting at the crowd to get back again. The roof was falling in. William jumped back quickly so as not to be trampled on by men who a moment ago were mouthing back to the officer.

The roof collapsed with a sigh. The wooden structure had been making loud cracking noises that had promised more of a dramatic fall. After each loud crack and creak the crowd collectively let out an *oooooohhhh!* When the wooden beams holding up the roof finally caved in, it could hardly be heard over the flames and the disappointed groans of the crowd. The firemen sprayed rainbows over Murray Street. The black and moss-green tiles smashed against the debris at the heart of the fire. The church spire still stood, facing forwards as if it had turned its back on the rubble.

— It's such a shame, innit? said Gladys from the Salvation Army shop a few doors down, to no one in particular. I used to go to Sunday school there when I was little. It survived the war and everything.

— Should have happened sooner, Gladys! said someone in the crowd.

This was the best day of William's summer so far. He had almost forgotten about his rejected story — he had a new story to write when he got home. The whole town had come out for the occasion. There was Jimmy Pugh, a can of Stella poking out of his breast pocket. A woman, looking like a slightly younger Kim Woodburn — his mum used to watch *How Clean Is Your House?* when he was a kid — with bleached hair and a green apron, was holding her pink-siliconed phone above the heads of the crowd in her clawed hand.

— Look! The roof has just gone in! she shouted into the mouthpiece.

— Yes, yes, I see it! said a girl on the other end in a thick Polish accent.

— Put your phone down, I can't see! someone yelled at her.

And there was Gary, not long out of rehab and apparently in talks to open his new business soon, scratching the stubble on his head, his hand on his son's shoulder. Looking past the many faces, William spotted his father. He was standing idly, his chin pointed upwards, brow furrowed, looking confused as to why the church was burning. William pushed through the crowd with many *thank yous* and *sorrys*, avoiding Danny Jenkins who was slumped against a lamp post.

— Alright, Dad? said William, by the side of him, causing his father to jump.

— Oh, alright, Will? Church is on fire, look. He pointed, as if William hadn't noticed. I was on my way to Spoons when I saw the smoke.

— Anyone know how it started?

— Some bloody kids, the police are saying.

They fell silent, together in the crowd, watching the firemen. More and more people joined them. William smiled to Chloe from his English class, the prettiest girl in college.

He'd crushed on her since the first year of secondary school. She smiled back, uncertainly, turned back to the fire. The metallic clip holding her hair back reflected the golden flames. Mr Owen from the *Llanelli Star* stood near the police cordon. He was scribbling furiously in a small pocketbook, bugging nearby spectators for statements. Nia Griffith was pushing her way through the crowd to get to the journalist, assuring people everything was fine and under control as she did so. William felt no jealousy, no bitterness nor rejection, watching the journalist write his notes and ask Nia for quotes. For the first time that summer he felt like something had happened to him, something that he could write about.

— I wish your grandfather was here to see this, William. He would have loved the community coming together like this.

When his father asked him if he wanted to go home, William said he wanted to stay longer. He stayed to write notes and observations on his phone until the sun set and the congregation of cygnets had dispersed, with nothing left to see. He stayed until the firemen drove off, and the fire was nothing but a smouldering pile of ash.

Acknowledgements

I'd first like to thank Claire Carroll and Andrew Mears for their thoughtful critique of my work, and for their friendship. No first draft gets written without it passing through them.

Thank you to the 2020 cohort of the Creative Writing MA at Bath Spa University, where I began to properly work on what would become *Local Fires*. The mentorship of the course staff was invaluable in my education as a writer.

Richard at Parthian Books chose to take a risk on me and these stories, for which I'm entirely grateful for. Thanks, too, to the wider Parthian team for all their hard work – especially Robert Harries, my designer, editor and occasional therapist, for believing in *Local Fires* and helping to make the stories the best they could be.

Thank you to the editors of the publications who have accepted stories from *Local Fires* and gave them their first home. I'd especially like to thank Dr Elaine Canning and her staff, guest editors Julia Bell (2021) and Jane Fraser (2023) for twice shortlisting me for the Rhys Davies Prize Award.

Thanks Mum, Dad and Dylan, all the people, places, traumas and memories that make up Llanelli – and the idea of 'home'.

I'd finally like to thank Rey Hope. I don't need to say why – you know why. Thank you.

Libraries Wales Author of the Month – Joshua Jones

1 What inspired you to write *Local Fires*?

I began writing *Local Fire*s in 2019, when I began my MA
in Creative Writing at Bath Spa University. Before then I
was mainly writing and performing poetry. I had wanted
to write prose for a long time, but I couldn't get over the
barrier. I felt, because of my autism and ADHD, which,
for me, comes with impatience and short attention span,
that I wouldn't be able to sit down and *write*.

When I did eventually begin writing the first stories that
would make up *Local Fires*, I was inspired by real memories
of my hometown, the people that live there and documented
my experiences growing up. The awkwardness of my
teenage years, experiences of toxic masculinity, casual
homophobia, the generational despair of a town emptied of
industry and employment.

2 Tell us a little about the book...

Local Fires is a collection of interconnected short stories,
all set in my hometown of Llanelli, South Wales. The
stories contain real streets, real events, that left a mark on
me growing up in the town. From the inertia of living in
an ex-industrial working-class area, to gender, sexuality,
toxic masculinity and neurodivergence, these stories are

hopefully versatile in themes and observations, and the town's inhabitants spill across the pages and into each other's stories. I think some of them are quite funny too!

3   What inspires you?

My own, disjointed memory of how I felt navigating growing up, and how I experience the world around me as a queer, neurodivergent person. I'm also interested in urban nature, displacement, psychogeography and the work of Mark Fisher. I always, always find inspiration in music – the first two offerings by Modest Mouse, for example, as well as Arab Strap and XIU XIU.

4   How did you know you wanted to be a writer and when?

My mum says I always wrote when I was young, but I can't remember, and I haven't seen much evidence of it. But I was a big reader since primary school – often getting in trouble because I refused to do my work, and wanted to read instead. I was actually punished for reading! I got into writing properly in college, especially poetry. I began performing spoken word in college after I discovered Arab Strap, whose vocalist, Aidan Moffat, primarily performs spoken word (and in a very strong Scots accent).

5   Can you name a few books that have left an impression on you?

James Joyce – *Dubliners*
Thomas Morris – *We Don't Know What We're Doing*
J. G. Ballard – *Crash*

Mark Fisher – *Ghosts of My Life*
Richard Foster – *Flower Factory*
A. M. Homes – *The Safety of Objects*
The completed plays of Sarah Kane
Dean Young's poetry
Queer Square Mile, edited by Kirsti Bohata, Mihangel Morgan and Huw Osborne

6   What would be some advice you would give to your younger self?
Be less self-protective, and more open. Listen more

7   What is your writing process?
Loud music, lots of coffee.

8   Do you enjoy other creative processes except for writing?
I like to make collage, and use experimental writing techniques including cut-up text. I have an occasional music project called Human Head. I also create installation art that utilises video, paint, sound, photography and found objects.

9   What books are currently on your bedside table?
So many! Far too many. But:
Yuko Tsushima – *Of Dogs and Wails*
Olivia Liang – *The Lonely City*
Patrick Keiller – *The View from the Train*
Iain Sinclair – *Living with Buildings*

10 In what way have libraries influenced you during your lifetime?

Llanelli library practically brought me up, according to my mother. I would get hyper-focussed on reading, I loved it so much, but we didn't have the money to keep up with the rate I read. Libraries are crucial to families with very little income. I would do all-nighters in the library when writing my third-year dissertation. When I visit a new city, I love to check out the library – when I went to Oslo last year on holiday, I spent an hour or two looking around the central library, which also had a bar/restaurant and a cinema!

11 Do you have suggestions of how to encourage children and young people to read more for pleasure?

There are so many fantastic writers and artists publishing work dedicated to queer, neurodivergent families and children, and people of colour. There is a world of informative, educational, and relatable books for children and young people. For example, *The Black Flamingo* by Dean Atta is written in poetic prose and tells the story of a young black boy who is gay, and finds himself through drag. Children and young people will read, they just need to be reached.

12 What are your plans for future titles?

I'm working on a collection of essays that further develop some of the themes and the ideas in *Local Fires*, and consider Mark Fisher's theories of hauntology. They also critically examine art or artists with a connection to my hometown, and cover themes of nostalgia, melancholia and memory.

Also, I am working with writers from Wales and Viet Nam to produce work on the themes of queerness, community and shared heritage, which will hopefully culminate in a printed publication, as part of the UK/VN season with the British Council.